Entangled Frequencies

A Platinum Chocolate Romance

By LongTemple

Entangled Frequencies – A Platinum Chocolate Romance

Published by Platinum Chocolate Publishing

Platinum Chocolate
PUBLISHING

An Independent Imprint of LongTemple

ISBN: 978-1-972217-22-1 (paperback)

Cover Design: LongTemple

Interior Layout: LongTemple

First Edition - Printed in the United States of America

10 9 8 7 6 5 4 3 2 1

Dedication:

For those who know that love is not found—it is recognized.

For the ones who listen when the frequency shifts,
who understand that connection is not about perfection,
but presence, timing, and the courage to stay.

For the women who hold each other steady while navigating love, ambition, and becoming.

For those who move with intention, love with awareness, and choose truth—even when it disrupts comfort.
This is for you.

Table of Contents

Chapter One: The Algorithm of Love

The city didn't sleep—it recalculated. It pulsed with data and desire, with signals crossing in the dark between people who were always connected and rarely touched.

Screens lit faces in dim apartments and passing cars, in corner cafés where conversations drifted between lips and pixels.

Love didn't just happen anymore. It was suggested. Filtered. Optimized and delivered like everything else—fast, efficient, curated. And still…it missed things.

Timing.

Energy.

The slow burn of a glance that lingered half a second too long.

Algorithms couldn't predict that.

Maya Reynolds knew that better than most, which was ironic, considering her entire career revolved around designing the very systems people trusted to tell them what they wanted.

Her laptop glowed against the amber hush of her apartment, lines of clean code stacked precisely across the screen. Six hours into refining a user flow, everything worked exactly the way it was supposed to.

And yet—

Her fingers hovered above the keyboard, not because she didn't know her next move, but because she was tired of fixing chaos for people who refused to admit they didn't know themselves.

Her phone buzzed.

She didn't look right away.

Another buzz.

The group chat always came alive at night—when defenses dropped and honesty slipped through humor without warning.

Maya leaned back in her chair, exhaled, and finally reached for her phone.

Group Chat: Frequency

Zaria: *I just signed up.*

Nia: *For what? Another app to ignore men on?*

Imani: *Wait... is this that Sync'd thing?*

Maya smirked, thumbs moving fast.

Maya: *Please don't tell me y'all fell for another "elite network of professionals" situation.*

Zaria: *Excuse you. Some of us are open to opportunity.*

Nia: *Opportunities to be annoyed.*

Imani: *I heard it's different. It connects based on habits, not just preferences.*

Maya rolled her eyes—and clicked the link anyway.

Sync'd.

The interface loaded smoothly, dark mode with gold accents, minimalist elegance that was almost irritating in how well it worked.

Whoever built this understood restraint and intention, and that alone made her pause.

A prompt appeared across the screen.

We don't match you with who you say you want.

We match you with who you move like.

Maya leaned in despite herself.

"That's dangerous," she murmured.

Her phone buzzed again, this time a voice note from Zaria.

Maya hit play, letting her friend's energy spill into the room.

"Listen... I don't know about y'all, but I'm tired of men who look good on paper and feel like drywall in real life. If this app can find somebody with an actual pulse, I'm trying it."

Maya laughed softly.

"Drywall is wild," she muttered.

Across the city, Zaria Barrett stood barefoot in her high-rise apartment, the skyline stretching beyond the glass as if it belonged to her.

Wine glass in hand, silk robe parted just enough to be intentional, she moved the way she always did—controlled, seductive, unbothered.

Sync'd waited in her palm.

She answered every question with ease; she knew how to curate desire.

Until one stopped her.

When do you feel most like yourself?

Her thumb hovered.

Then: *When I'm not performing.*

She stared at the answer longer than necessary before pressing submit.

Imani Clarke sat at her kitchen table, everything exactly where it belonged—tea steaming, phone upright, posture composed.

She read each question twice, not from uncertainty but from respect.

Truth mattered, even when it complicated things. Especially then.

The final question appeared.

What are you afraid someone will discover about you?

Her jaw tightened.

That I want more than I pretend I do.

She submitted it and immediately set the phone aside, pulse steady but alert, as if she'd just revealed too much skin.

And then there was Nia.

Nia Jackson didn't linger.

Scrubs half unzipped, shoes abandoned by the door, she leaned against her counter while Sync'd loaded, answering on instinct—swipe, answer, skip.

Until—

What do you do when something starts to feel real?

She stopped chewing, read it again, then laughed—low and knowing.

"Exit," she said out loud, tapping the screen.

Back in her apartment, Maya completed the last question without registering how long she'd been sitting still.

She closed the app and tossed her phone aside, stretching as tension pulled through her shoulders.

"Another algorithm," she said quietly.

Her body didn't agree.

Not the design.

Not the questions.

Something about the intent lingered—subtle and persistent.

Her phone buzzed again.

Group Chat: Frequency

Zaria: *So we're all doing this, right?*

Nia: *Speak for yourself.*

Imani: *I already finished.*

Maya stared at the screen longer than necessary before typing.

Maya: *I'll try it. But I'm not expecting anything.*

Zaria: *That's why you're single.*

Maya: *And peaceful.*

Nia: *And bored.*

Maya smiled.

Maya: *Debatable.*

Across the city, four profiles finalized within minutes of each other.

Four women moving through separate rooms.

Separate moods.

Separate nights.

System Update Complete.

Matches pending.

Not based on what they wanted—but on how they moved.

Maya's phone lit up again. A notification this time.

Sync'd: You've been matched.

She didn't open it.

Didn't move.

She just sat there, screen glowing softly against the wall, aware of her breath in a way she hadn't been a moment before—heart steady, something unfamiliar warming beneath her skepticism.

Across the city, three other phones lit up.

Nothing ended.

Nothing resolved.

But somewhere between one breath and the next, something quiet had started to shift.

Chapter Two: The Worst Blind Date Ever

Maya did not open the notification that night.

She saw it.

She felt it.

And then she shut down her laptop without touching her phone, moving through her apartment with practiced calm—intentional, measured, the kind of restraint she relied on when she did not want to name what was happening.

Her phone rested on the couch, faceup, inconveniently present.

She ignored it longer than she meant to.

Long enough for irritation to bleed into curiosity.

Long enough for curiosity to turn into something sharper.

Eventually, she turned back, picked it up, and opened Sync'd.

The interface did not rush her. No pulsing animations.

No exaggerated enthusiasm. Just a clean screen, patient and unbothered.

You've been matched.

A name followed.

Andre Coleman

No headline. No clever hook. Just three lines:

Cybersecurity Analyst.

Observes more than he speaks.

Doesn't entertain nonsense.

Maya blinked once.

"Sir... who asked you to come in this direct?" she murmured.

She tapped further into the profile. Minimal.

No posed smiles. No *caught-in-the-moment* energy.

Just one photo—Andre leaning against a rooftop railing at night, city lights blurred behind him.

Calm.

Still.

Unreadable.

Maya narrowed her gaze.

"Oh. You're one of those."

Her thumb hovered.

Then—

A message appeared.

Andre: So this is what the algorithm thinks I need?

Maya laughed, short and sharp.

"Oh, we're starting strong."

Her fingers moved before she reconsidered.

Maya: *I was thinking the same thing.*

The typing indicator appeared.

Vanished.

Returned.

She leaned back slightly.

Andre: *Good. At least we agree on something.*

Maya exhaled through her nose.

Maya: *Don't get comfortable.*

A pause.

Andre: *Wasn't planning to.*

Her smile stayed longer than she expected it to.

Across the city, Andre sat at his desk, three monitors glowing—code on one, security logs scrolling on another, Maya's profile open on the third.

He leaned back in his chair, eyes lingering on the empty spaces.

"She's going to argue," he said quietly.

His phone buzzed.

Maya: *So what exactly did this app pick up on? Because I'm not seeing it yet.*

The corner of his mouth shifted.

Andre: *Probably that we both think we're the smartest person in the room.*

Maya stared at the message.

Maya: *Oh, you're funny.*

Andre: *No. I'm accurate.*

She laughed—once, quick, then softer.

Two days later, Maya met him anyway.

The restaurant was dim and controlled, the kind of place that let conversations drop without forcing intimacy.

She arrived early, claimed her seat, adjusted her sleeve, checked her phone without opening anything.

Two minutes past the hour, a shadow crossed the table.

"No hug?"

She looked up.

Andre.

In person, he did not loom; he settled.

No excess movement.

No effort to impress.

"We don't know each other," she said.

He pulled out the chair across from her and sat.

"Fair."

Silence followed—not awkward, just waiting.

The waiter approached.

"Can I start you with something to drink?"

"Water's fine," Andre said.

"Same," Maya added.

When the waiter left, the quiet returned.

Andre's gaze flicked briefly to her hand, where one finger tapped against the glass before stilling.

"You always this conversational?" she asked.

"Only when there's something worth saying."

She laughed under her breath.

"Oh, this is going to be interesting."

"Only if you let it."

She leaned forward slightly.

"Let me guess. You think silence is depth."

Andre held her gaze, unhurried.

"No. I just don't speak to fill space."

She studied him for a beat, then leaned back.

"Alright."

"Respect."

Dinner moved without apology for small talk.

Questions surfaced, then receded.

"You don't think like that," Andre said at one point.

Maya paused.

"Excuse me?"

"You're editing yourself."

Her eyes narrowed.

"You don't know how I process."

Andre took a slow sip of water.

"I know enough."

She crossed her arms.

"You're one of those."

"One of what?"

"The ones who think they can read people quickly."

"I don't read," he said. *"I observe."*

Maya smiled despite herself.

"You're a lot."

"And you aren't?"

The words landed and stayed there.

Outside, the city pressed in, louder than the restaurant.

"We survived," Maya said.

"Barely."

She smiled, then let it stand.

"That wasn't awful."

"Low expectations help."

She laughed.

"Don't ruin it."

A pause stretched between them.

"I'll see you around," she said.

Andre did not stop her.

Did not reach.

"Yeah," he said. *"You will."*

Maya walked away without looking back, her steps steady, her thoughts tangled.

Andre watched her go a moment longer than necessary, then turned away.

Across the city, other nights continued.

This one did not settle into clarity.

It lingered.

Chapter Three: Spilled Coffee, Stolen Attention

Zaria Barrett did not believe in small entrances—not because she craved attention, but because she understood energy, the way a room responded when someone entered with purpose, the way control could be felt before it was spoken. Tonight mattered.

The venue crowned the top floor of a glass-wrapped building, the skyline stretched wide behind it like a promise, soft lighting tracing polished surfaces while curated music hummed beneath conversation.

Every element—from the floral installations to the digital check-in kiosks—bore Zaria's unmistakable signature: controlled, elevated, seamless.

At least—that was the intention.

"Why is that screen lagging?"

Her voice was low and precise as she crossed the floor with her tablet in hand, heels striking with authority.

A staff member hurried beside her. *"We're fixing it now—just a slight delay in the—"*

"No," Zaria interrupted, her gaze already tracking the issue. *"Not slight. Noticeable. Fix it."*

She didn't slow. Zaria didn't do panic—she did pressure, and pressure, when applied correctly, made things shine.

Across the room, Malik Thompson noticed her without meaning to—not because she demanded attention, but because the environment adjusted around her. People shifted, listened, made space.

Malik reclined slightly in his chair, laptop open, code scrolling steadily across the screen as his focus sharpened.

"That's her," someone murmured nearby.

He didn't ask who. He already knew.

Zaria Barrett.

He studied her movements with impartial focus—not interest, not admiration, but assessment. She carried weight the way others carried accessories, and no one carried weight effortlessly.

"Malik."

He didn't look up.

"Yeah."

"The check-in system is glitching again."

That earned his attention. He closed his laptop halfway, eyes narrowing slightly.

"It's not glitching," he said evenly. *"It's compensating."*

The staff member blinked. *"Compensating for what?"*

Malik stood, tucking the laptop under his arm. *"Too many last-minute changes."*

He was already moving.

Zaria approached the check-in station with singular focus, her mind calculating fixes in real time. *"Why is this still—"*

Impact. Hot. Sharp. Liquid.

Coffee spilled across cream silk.

"—not fixed?" Her voice faltered as she looked down.

The blouse was ruined, brown spreading where polish had been intention, and for one suspended second, Zaria went completely still.

Then she lifted her gaze.

Malik stood there, empty cup in hand—calm, unrattled, unapologetic. Bold.

"You ran into me," he said calmly.

Zaria blinked. Once. Twice.

"Excuse me?" Her voice dropped—quiet, surgical.

"You were moving quickly," Malik continued, as if explaining circuitry. *"I was stationary."*

She stared at him.

The nerve. The composure.

"You spilled coffee on me," she said slowly.

"You collided with me," he corrected.

A beat passed. People nearby began to notice.

Zaria exhaled once, sharp and controlled. *"Do you work for me?"*

"No."

She stepped forward, closing the space just enough. *"Then let me be clear,"* she said evenly. *"When something like this happens at my event, you apologize. You don't debate physics."*

Malik met her gaze—really saw her.

Then—*"You're right."*

She paused.

"I should have led with that," he continued, voice steady. *"My fault."*

The tension shifted.

Zaria studied him, measuring sincerity, then stepped back. *"Thank you."*

She brushed at the blouse—futile.

A staff member appeared with napkins. *"Ms. Barrett—"*

"I'm fine," she said, her eyes never leaving Malik.

Now she was registering him—not the mistake, not the moment, but the man who didn't scramble, didn't fold.

"The system's lagging because the guest list was updated after initial load," Malik said, nodding toward the screen.

She turned, then back to him. *"And you know this how?"*

"I built it."

That landed.

You're Malik," she said.

Yeah."

The air changed.

Five minutes later, they stood shoulder to shoulder—her blouse still ruined, his hands moving across the keyboard with quiet mastery.

"You pushed a live update without rebalancing the queue," he said.

"I didn't push anything," Zaria replied. *"My team did."*

"Your team follows your direction."

She tilted her head slightly. *"You always this direct?"*

"Only when accuracy matters."

She huffed softly. *"There's a pattern here."*

"Yeah?"

"Men explaining my event to me."

He glanced at her. *"I'm explaining the system, not critiquing you."*

She watched him for a beat, then—*"Fix it."*

"Already doing that."

The adjustments were fast, precise. The screen smoothed. Flow restored.

Zaria nodded once. *"That'll work."*

"It'll hold," Malik said, closing his laptop.

She looked down at her blouse, then back up. *"You owe me a replacement."*

corner of his mouth lifted. *"That can be arranged."*

"Good," she said lightly. *"This wasn't inexpensive."*

"I noticed," he replied. *"You don't cut corners."*

That earned him a look—and then a smile, small and unguarded.

The evening continued flawlessly, but Zaria found herself tracking him—where he stood, how he watched, the way he never reached for attention.

Malik noticed, too. He didn't interrupt it, didn't label it. He just stayed present.

Later, as the crowd thinned, Zaria approached again—deliberate now.

"You stayed."

"I wanted to be sure it held."

She nodded. *"Thank you."* This time, it meant more.

"You're welcome."

A pause.

"Next time," she said, adjusting her sleeve, *"aim away from the wardrobe."*

He almost smiled.

"Next time—watch your stride."

She laughed, didn't hide it, and as she walked away, something lingered—not excitement, not yet, but disruption.

Because sometimes, the right connection didn't arrive smoothly.

It collided.

Chapter Four: Profile vs. Reality

Imani Clarke did not believe in illusions—not in business, not in numbers, and absolutely never in men who looked too good on paper.

That was why she'd taken her time with Sync'd.

She hadn't skimmed or rushed, hadn't allowed herself to be seduced by clever phrasing or curated charm, because she knew patterns lived in details—and details always confessed the truth before people did.

She read everything twice, deliberately, methodically, with the quiet confidence of someone who trusted her instincts because she trained them.

So when Devon Harris appeared on her screen…

She paused.

Not because he was impressive—but because he wasn't trying to be.

His profile was restrained, structured, confident without posturing.

Founder. Tech strategist. Builder of scalable systems. Believes in growth—but not at the expense of peace. Enjoys quiet spaces, good food, and conversations that evolve.

Imani leaned back slightly. *"Interesting."*

The photos followed the same logic: one at a conference—natural, not posed; one candid smile that didn't feel rehearsed; one understated setting that didn't beg to be admired. Balanced.

Which, in her experience, usually meant curated with care.

Her phone vibrated.

Devon: *You read profiles like reports, don't you?*

Imani blinked. Then smiled—slow, deliberate.

Imani: *Only when they read like executive summaries.*

A pause. Then—

Devon: *So I passed the first filter?*

She crossed one leg over the other before answering.

Imani: *You weren't dismissed immediately.*

Devon: *I'll take it.*

Across the city, Devon reclined at his desk—sleek, intentional, expensive-looking in a way that suggested momentum rather than permanence.

His laptop was open, phone tilted in his hand, a glass of amber liquid resting near his right side like punctuation rather than indulgence.

He reread her response once, then again.

"She's not the easy kind," he murmured—not a complaint, but a preference.

His thumb hovered before typing.

Devon: *What gets you through the second filter?*

Imani read the message and set the phone down, because she didn't respond on impulse. She rewarded consistency, not urgency.

She stood, poured fresh water for her tea, watched the steam curl upward, then returned to the table before replying.

Imani: *Consistency.*

Devon leaned back, a slow smile forming. Their conversations unfolded without pressure. They didn't rush—they built.

Imani asked questions most people avoided, questions about failure and pressure and what success looked like when no one was applauding.

Devon answered well—not flawlessly, but convincingly.

He talked about scaling systems, managing growth, investor expectations, long nights and strategic risk.

He knew the cadence, the language, the confidence of someone almost arrived.

Because for Devon, truth wasn't always about accuracy. Sometimes, it was about presentation.

Three days later, they agreed to meet.

The restaurant was intimate—quiet but not empty, refined without pretension.

Imani arrived exactly on time, no advantage given and no moment surrendered. She scanned the room once before spotting him.

Devon stood immediately. Good. She appreciated awareness.

"You're Imani," he said, his voice smooth without leaning into charm.

"I am."

Up close, he matched expectation: well-groomed, controlled posture, presence that had been practiced—but not performed.

He pulled out her chair.

She sat.

"Thank you."

"You're welcome."

Appropriate. Correct.

The first ten minutes moved exactly as they should—polite, easy, neutral—until Imani leaned forward slightly.

"Tell me about your company."

Devon smiled once and settled in. *"Tech consulting. We optimize systems, scale infrastructure, and build platforms that sustain pressure."*

She listened to cadence more than content.

"What stage are you in?"

"Growth."

Vague. Noted.

"How many clients?"

"Enough to stay busy."

She tilted her head. *"That's not a number."*

A smile. *"Intentional."*

She held his gaze. *"Why?"*

The air shifted. Devon leaned back, tapping once against the table.

"Because numbers create expectations that don't always align with reality."

Imani didn't blink. *"Or,"* she said evenly, *"they expose it."*

A beat. Then his smile returned—smaller now.

"You're sharp."

"I pay attention."

Dinner arrived and the conversation deepened, moving now with push and counter, precision and pause.

Devon answered everything she asked, but some details drifted—nothing glaring, nothing loud.

Just misalignment. And Imani clocked every one.

Halfway through the meal, she set her fork down.

"Earlier you said you were in meetings all day," she noted calmly, *"but you also mentioned hands-on development this week."*

Devon paused, then recovered. *"Depends on the day."*

She nodded—and pressed. *"Which was it today?"*

Silence stretched. Devon exhaled and set his fork down. *"A bit of both."*

She watched him carefully. *"Okay."*

But something had shifted—not broken, just exposed.

Outside, the city breathed quieter as they stood facing each other, close enough for awareness and distant enough for control.

"I enjoyed this," Devon said.

"I did too."

Despite everything, it was true.

"You're different from what I expected."

"How so?"

He considered her. *"More precise."*

She smiled faintly. *"That's one word."*

He stepped closer—not invasion, just presence.

"And you? Am I what you expected?"

She paused, because she didn't lie to herself.

"You're... interesting."

He laughed. *"That sounds like an ongoing review."*

"It is."

As she walked away, Imani didn't replay every exchange. She didn't dissect or spiral, because one truth was already clear.

Devon Harris was not exactly who he presented—but he wasn't a fabrication either. He was curated, controlled, and flawed enough to be human.

Behind her, Devon watched her go, jaw set and thoughts unsettled, because he understood something now: Imani Clarke would not accept illusion for long.

Which meant—at some point—he'd have to decide how much truth he was ready to reveal.

And whether she would stay—when he did.

Chapter Five: One Night, No Names

Nia Jackson didn't go out to be found. She went out to forget.

The rooftop pulsed with curated chaos—city lights spilling across glass and steel, music low enough to press against the body instead of overpowering it, conversations rising and falling in smooth currents of laughter and intimacy that felt practiced rather than accidental. It wasn't her usual scene.

Nia didn't belong to places like this; she passed through them, left before anything could settle long enough to attach.

Her scrubs were gone, replaced with clean lines and restraint—nothing flashy, nothing pleading for attention, nothing that asked to be remembered.

Her hair was pulled back just enough to frame her face without asking to be touched, and everything about her posture, her presence, her stillness said *contained.*

She leaned against the bar, waiting for her drink, eyes observant without settling, letting the room move around her without engaging it.

Observe. Don't engage unless necessary. Don't stay long enough for anything to attach.

"Tequila?"

She didn't turn right away.

"Depends who's asking."

"Someone who's already ordering it."

That made her look.

Jordan.

Tall. Composed. Dressed with the same quiet precision she favored—no performance, no excess, presence without intrusion.

He didn't smile immediately, and she noticed that first; the second thing she noticed was that he wasn't trying.

The bartender slid two glasses across the counter, and Jordan nudged one toward her.

"Just in case."

She glanced at the glass, then at him, then lifted it.

"Just in case."

They drank.

No introductions. No toast. Just mutual acknowledgment that didn't ask for explanation.

Minutes slipped by—not awkward, not heavy, just present in a way that resisted definition.

"You don't come out often," he said.

It wasn't a question.

She rested one shoulder into the bar. *"You don't know that."*

A faint shrug. *"I know enough."*

A breath left her that nearly became a laugh. *"Everyone's perceptive tonight."*

"What does that mean?"

She turned slightly toward him now, just enough to acknowledge the exchange. *"It means people keep thinking they can read me."*

He held her gaze. *"I didn't say I could."*

"You implied it."

A nod. *"Fair."*

Then—

"You don't stay long."

That landed closer than she liked. She didn't answer, just sipped, letting the space sit where it fell.

"You talk a lot for someone who just met me."

He tilted his head. *"You're still here."*

Simple. Unavoidable. True.

"You always this confident?"

"Only when I'm right."

A smile slipped free—brief, unguarded, gone.

They didn't exchange names, not because they forgot, but because they chose not to.

The music slowed, deeper now, heavier, and Jordan extended a hand—no drama, no presumption, just an offer made without pressure.

"Dance?"

She studied him once more, then placed her hand in his.

The dance was restrained and measured, close enough to feel heat, far enough to keep control. His hand settled at her back, steady and deliberate, not claiming—just present.

She leaned in only enough to acknowledge connection.

"You think too much," he murmured.

"You don't know what I'm thinking."

"I know you're trying not to."

That—**that**—came too close.

She shifted back slightly. *"You do this with everyone?"*

"Do what?"

"Act like you already know them."

He considered it. *"No."*

She searched for an angle and didn't find one, and that unsettled her more than charm ever could.

Hours later, the rooftop had thinned, the energy softened into the kind of night that either ended quietly—or moved somewhere private.

She stood near the exit, already halfway gone, when Jordan approached without urgency.

"You leaving?"

"Yeah."

A pause.

"Come with me."

Not persuasion. Not demand. A statement left open by intention.

She evaluated him carefully. This was familiar geography—temporary, contained, clean.

"You don't even know my name."

A faint curve touched his mouth. *"Didn't seem necessary."*

She held his gaze. Then—

"Okay."

His place made sense. Minimal. Orderly. No distractions. A space built for control rather than display.

She slipped off her shoes.

"You live alone."

"Yeah."

A nod. *"Figures."*

The door closed behind them, locked out of habit, with nothing rushed and everything intentional.

A held breath. A glance that lingered. A step closer that didn't need permission.

His hand brushed hers—light, questioning.

She didn't pull away, didn't lean in, let timing decide.

Then she closed the space.

Later, the room held quiet instead of absence, city glow tracing shadows across stillness that felt suspended rather than finished.

She sat at the edge of the bed, dressing with practiced efficiency, while Jordan watched her without assumption.

"You always leave like this?"

"Yeah."

A pause.

"You always ask questions afterward?"

A soft exhale. *"Not always."*

She finished dressing, then looked at him. *"For what it's worth—this was exactly what I needed."*

Clear. Contained.

He sat up. *"For what it's worth—it didn't feel like just that."*

There it was, the complication she refused to acknowledge.

"That's where I exit."

She slipped on her shoes.

"No names."

A nod. *"No names."*

Her hand paused at the door just long enough to feel the weight of it, then she left.

The hallway was quiet, the city still pulsing beyond it. Nia didn't look back—because that was her rule.

Inside, Jordan leaned back, breath slow, unsettled, because some connections were never meant to be clean.

Across the city, four stories had begun—different, unbalanced, unpredictable.

And one of them was never supposed to last past sunrise.

But it would.

Chapter Six: Group Chat Chaos

The group chat didn't just exist—it lived, activating in the quiet moments when the world slowed just enough for truth to surface through sarcasm, humor, and the kind of honesty that only happened between women who trusted each other enough not to perform.

Maya's phone buzzed against the couch as she sank into it, one leg tucked beneath her, her laptop still open on the coffee table and completely forgotten as her mind drifted—half on unfinished work, half on a date that hadn't gone badly but hadn't gone easily either.

She picked up her phone without hurry. She already knew. The chat was active.

Zaria had started it—again, predictably, decisively.

Zaria: *I need everyone present and accounted for because tonight was NOT normal.*

Maya exhaled through her nose, adjusting her position.

Maya: *Define "not normal," because your life is chaos by design.*

Typing bubbles popped up immediately—overlapping, colliding.

Nia: *If this is about another man, I'm already tired.*

Zaria: *First of all, don't start. Second of all—yes, but also no.*

A beat passed before Imani entered—not rushed, not loud, just intentional.

Imani *That response doesn't inspire confidence.*

Maya smiled, settling deeper into the couch.

Maya: *Alright. Who's going first? Because I have thoughts.*

Zaria: *No. I'm going first because I almost fought a man at my own event.*

That captured everyone. Even Nia.

Nia: *Oh. Now I'm listening.*

Maya sat up.

Maya: *You almost WHAT?*

A voice note followed, and Maya hit play immediately, already picturing Zaria pacing mid-rant.

"Listen... when I say this man spilled coffee on me, I don't mean a little spill. I mean full, disrespectful, outfit-ruining, right-before-the-event

coffee. AND THEN—he had the nerve to tell me I ran into him."

Maya laughed out loud.

Nia: *I would've dragged him.*

Imani: *Immediately.*

Maya: *Publicly.*

Another voice note came through—same heat, different undertone.

"That's what I'm saying! But then he apologized. Calm. Like it didn't shake him at all. And I hated that. I don't like when people don't react the way they're supposed to."

Maya smiled slightly. She read that perfectly.

Maya: *You didn't like that he didn't give you control of the moment.*

Typing stopped. Then—

Zaria: *Do NOT psychoanalyze me right now.*

Maya: *I'm not. I'm accurate.*

Nia: *Here we go.*

Imani followed—steady, neutral, direct.

Imani: *What happened after the apology?*

Silence stretched. Then—

Zaria: *He fixed my system.*

The chat froze. Then—

Maya: *Oh. You like him.*

Nia: *Yeah, it's already over for you.*

Zaria: *I DO NOT LIKE HIM.*

Maya grinned.

Maya: *You said he stayed calm, challenged you, and solved your problem. That's your type.*

Zaria: *That is NOT my type.*

Nia: *That is exactly your type.*

Maya leaned back, laughing.

Imani: *What's his name?*

A pause.

Zaria: *Malik.*

Maya raised a brow.

Maya: *That sounds like a man who wins arguments quietly.*

Nia: *Yeah... the dangerous kind.*

Zaria: *I hate all of you.*

Maya: *You love us.*

The energy shifted—naturally, instinctively—as Nia didn't announce her story so much as slide it into the moment.

Nia: *I met someone.*

Typing bubbles erupted.

Maya: *And?*

Zaria: *AND???*

Imani: *Details.*

Nia waited. Then—

NIA: *It was nothing.*

Maya immediately sat up. No one bought that.

Zaria: *If it was nothing, you wouldn't have said anything.*

Nia: *It was just a night.*

Maya: *You don't mention "just nights."*

A pause followed. Then—

Nia: *We didn't exchange names.*

That landed hard.

Imani: *That was intentional.*

Maya: *That was avoidance.*

Nia: *That was peace.*

Maya softened—she recognized that tone.

Maya: *Did you want to stay?*

Typing… stopped. Started. Stopped again. Then—

Nia: *That's not the point.*

Maya: *That's exactly the point.*

Silence followed, thick and telling, before Nia redirected the way she always did when something got too close.

Nia: *Anyway. I left. End of story.*

None of them believed that.

Imani waited before speaking, because her story required precision.

Imani: *I met mine too.*

Maya focused.

Maya: *And?*

Zaria: *Don't go vague now.*

Nia: *Full report.*

Imani exhaled slowly.

Imani: *He isn't completely honest.*

Everything paused.

Maya: *Already?*

Zaria: *How do you know?*

Nia: *What did he lie about?*

Imani: *Not lie. Adjust.*

Maya frowned.

Maya: *That's worse.*

Zaria: *Much worse.*

Nia: *That means he's strategic.*

Imani: *Exactly.*

Then—

Maya: *Do you like him?*

Imani hesitated, because that mattered.

Imani: *I'm still deciding.*

All attention shifted to Maya.

Zaria: *Alright, Ms. "I Don't Expect Anything." What happened on your date?*

Maya leaned back.

Maya: *It was… not easy.*

Nia: *That's bad.*

Maya: *It wasn't bad.*

Zaria: *That's worse.*

Maya smiled faintly.

Maya: *It was honest.*

That quieted everyone.

Imani: *How?*

Maya: *He doesn't fill space. Doesn't perform. Doesn't need to be liked.*

Nia: *That's dangerous.*

Zaria: *That's how they get under your skin.*

Maya swallowed.

Maya: *His name is Andre.*

A beat.

Zaria: *Yeah… you're done.*

Maya: *Relax.*

Nia: *No, seriously. You're irritated and intrigued already.*

Maya smiled.

Maya: *I am.*

They laughed—even Imani—and the chat slowed, not because there was nothing left to say, but because everything that mattered had been acknowledged.

Four women. Four connections. One city. One shift.

Maya set her phone aside, eyes drifting back to her laptop without focus.

Across the city, Zaria stared at a faint stain on her blouse, Imani reviewed instincts she trusted, and Nia stood at her window with her arms crossed, something familiar and unresolved pressing close.

Because some connections didn't arrive loudly.

They settled quietly.

Then stayed.

Chapter Seven: The Second Chance Date

Maya told herself she wasn't going to overthink it—which, for her, meant she already had, thoroughly and methodically, from at least six angles before pretending she hadn't.

Her phone rested on the kitchen counter as she stood stirring nothing, the spoon clinking softly against ceramic while her attention drifted back to the same unasked question.

Why say yes again.

It lingered without resolution, irritating in its simplicity.

The first date hadn't been smooth.

Andre hadn't charmed her, hadn't eased anything into comfort, and there was nothing predictable about the way the evening had unfolded.

He hadn't filled space or softened edges, and she hadn't decided whether that unsettled her or drew her in.

She'd said yes before she could reframe it.

Her phone buzzed.

She didn't rush, but she didn't avoid it either, lifting it only once she was ready to acknowledge the pull.

Andre: *Same place. Less tension this time.*

Maya stared at the screen, then smirked.

Maya: *Don't make promises you can't keep.*

A pause.

Then—

Andre: *I don't make promises.*

She shook her head, a quiet laugh escaping.

The restaurant hadn't changed.

The lighting was the same, the layout familiar, the atmosphere exactly as deliberate as before.

What felt different was her—how she stepped inside without scanning the room, how she didn't chart exits or orient herself before moving forward.

Andre was already there.

He noticed her immediately, standing as she approached—not to impress, nothing rehearsed, just a shift of attention that registered before she did.

"You're on time."

She tilted her head.

"I usually am."

"I figured."

She slid into her seat, movements precise.

"You're early."

"I don't like rushing."

She studied him, a faint smile touching her mouth.

"That tracks."

The silence settled easily this time.

Not filled. Not avoided.

Glasses were set down, menus briefly opened and closed, the space between them unforced but attentive.

Maya rested her fingers near her glass.

"So," she said, *"what made you agree to a second date?"*

Andre didn't answer right away.

He didn't dodge or soften it, just held her gaze for a beat longer than necessary.

"You didn't try to impress me."

She blinked.

"That's your bar?"

"It's rare."

She leaned back slightly.

"Most people perform," he added. *"You didn't."*

Her mouth pressed into a thin line.

"I didn't feel like I needed to."

He nodded.

"Exactly."

She watched him more closely after that.

No rush. No adjustment to be easier. No effort to smooth perception.

"Do you always talk like this?" she asked.

"Like what?"

"Like everything's already filtered for truth."

"It is."

She laughed softly.

"That sounds exhausting."

"It removes confusion."

She tilted her head.

"Or creates tension."

"That too."

Their food arrived, and the conversation moved without resetting—direct, layered, unedited.

Maya spoke the way she thought, without simplifying herself, and Andre followed without interruption.

At some point, he said—

"You like control."

Her fork paused midair.

"Excuse me?"

"You structure everything," he said evenly. *"Work. Conversations. Outcomes."*

She set the fork down carefully.

"That's intention."

"It is," he agreed, *"but it's also control."*

She held his gaze.

"And you don't control?"

"Only what matters."

She leaned back a fraction.

"And the rest?"

"I let it be."

Her expression shifted, not breaking, just recalibrating.

"Nice in theory," she said quietly. *"Life doesn't always cooperate."*

"Neither does control."

The air changed—subtly, not sharply.

Outside, the night carried a different weight. Louder. Cooler. Uninterested in resolution.

They stood closer this time—not touching, not distant, aligned without deciding to be.

"This was... better," Maya said.

"It was."

"Less tension?"

Andre considered that.

"Different tension."

She smiled.

Silence followed—not empty, just alert.

"You almost kissed me earlier," Andre said.

Her head snapped toward him.

"I did not."

"You leaned in."

"I shifted."

"You held eye contact."

"That's normal."

"You didn't break it."

She stared at him, then laughed—full, unguarded.

"Wow. You really track everything."

"Patterns matter."

She stepped closer without planning to.

"And what pattern do you see?"

Andre didn't answer immediately.

"You don't do anything halfway."

Her smile softened, then stalled.

"That's not always a strength."

"No," he said. *"But it's honest."*

The space between them narrowed.

Her breath slowed. Her eyes dipped to his mouth, then lifted again. She didn't step back this time—but she didn't close the distance either.

Andre stayed where he was.

Waiting.

She felt it—pressure without pursuit.

And that unsettled her.

Maya stepped back first, the decision quiet but unmistakable.

"I should go."

Andre didn't reach for her.

"Okay."

She paused, then turned away.

The walk felt longer than it should have.

She didn't replay the conversation all at once—only fragments.

A look. A pause.

Something he hadn't said.

Behind her, Andre remained where she'd left him, hands in his pockets, expression unreadable.

Neither of them named what hadn't happened.

Neither of them closed it.

And the night moved on without resolution.

Chapter Eight: You Again

Zaria Barrett did not like repetition when it came to men. Systems? Absolutely. Events? Required it. Structure thrived on repetition. But people—no.

When the same man reappeared without planning, it meant something had slipped, and Zaria did not tolerate slippage.

So when she stepped into the conference room and saw Malik already seated—laptop open, posture calm, as if he had settled into the space rather than occupied it—she stopped just inside the doorway.

Not dramatically. Just enough.

"You again."

Malik looked up, gaze steady, unsurprised.

"Yeah."

She stepped fully inside, heels measured, tablet tucked beneath her arm as her posture shifted instinctively—professional, controlled, prepared.

"This is my meeting."

He nodded once, closing his laptop halfway before reopening it, unmoved.

"I know."

Zaria placed her tablet on the table with deliberate precision.

"Then why are you here?"

"Because the client asked for me."

His tone didn't rise or soften, didn't adjust for her authority, and that—annoyingly—didn't irritate her the way it should have.

She exhaled slowly.

The same man who'd disrupted her event and corrected it without fanfare was now embedded directly in her professional space.

"Of course they did," she murmured.

A corner of his mouth shifted.

"You say that like it's a problem."

She looked at him fully now.

"It's not a problem," she said evenly. *"It's a complication."*

Malik leaned back slightly.

"Those usually are."

"Not if you know how to manage them."

The meeting moved forward despite the unresolved tension. Clients filled the room, screens lit, conversations layered as Zaria took control immediately.

"Our goal is to streamline user experience while maintaining engagement flow," she said, gesturing toward the presentation. *"The last event highlighted delays we've identified and—"*

"It wasn't the event."

Her words paused—not broken, but interrupted.

Zaria turned slowly.

"I'm sorry?"

Malik didn't rush.

"It wasn't the event," he repeated. *"It was the system integration."*

The room noticed—not loudly, but enough.

Zaria smiled, polished and seamless.

"The integration is part of the event."

He shook his head once.

"No. It supports it."

There it was—that same refusal to let inaccuracies sit comfortably.

Zaria held his gaze a beat longer than necessary, then continued.

"As I was saying," she said smoothly, *"we've addressed the issue moving forward."*

Malik didn't interrupt again. He didn't need to.

When the room cleared, Zaria remained. She always did. Malik stayed too. She gathered her things without haste before speaking.

"You like correcting people."

Not a question.

"I like precision."

"You could've waited."

"For what?"

"For literally any moment that didn't involve contradicting me in front of clients."

He stood, shifting the energy without raising his voice.

"If something's wrong in real time, I address it."

She crossed her arms loosely.

"That's not always how business works."

"It is when outcomes matter more than perception."

That landed. She absorbed it.

"And respect?"

"Respect isn't silence," he replied. *"It's honesty."*

Zaria stared at him—not angry, assessing—as she exhaled slowly and recalibrated.

"You're difficult."

His mouth curved faintly.

"So are you."

She almost smiled. Almost.

They reached the door together. Zaria paused, her hand resting on the handle.

"You're not going to apologize, are you?"

He shook his head.

"No."

She nodded.

"Good."

That caught his attention.

"Good?"

She opened the door, then turned back.

"I don't need agreement," she said evenly. *"I need consistency."*

He studied her, then nodded.

"I can do that."

She held his gaze a moment longer.

"And try not to spill anything on me next time."

His almost-smile returned.

"No promises."

She shook her head, stepping into the hall.

"Of course not."

As Zaria walked away, her posture remained controlled, but her thoughts did not settle, because Malik Thompson didn't adapt to make things easier—and that didn't fit neatly into her system.

Which was a problem.

Behind her, Malik watched her go, his focus drifting beyond the professional, because Zaria Barrett didn't just manage rooms—she controlled them. And somehow, he had stepped into one she didn't fully command.

And neither of them seemed interested in leaving it.

Chapter Nine: Curated Truths

Imani Clarke didn't rush conclusions. She collected them—layer by layer, detail by detail—because patterns revealed themselves long before they announced meaning, and precision, to her, wasn't coldness; it was protection.

Which was why Devon Harris remained deliberately unresolved: not accepted, not dismissed, but observed with intention rather than assumption.

Her phone rested beside her laptop as she worked through a dataset, the muted hum of her apartment usually grounding her.

Tonight, though, her attention drifted just enough to notice his name lingering among her recent messages, the cadence of their exchanges replaying without invitation.

Her screen lit.

Devon: *You always working this late?*

Imani finished the calculation she was adjusting, saved the file, closed the window—then reached for her phone.

Imani: *I always finish what I start.*

The response came quickly.

Devon: *That sounds like a rule.*

She leaned back, crossing one leg over the other.

Imani: *It is.*

A pause followed.

Devon: *That must make life predictable.*

Her brow lifted slightly.

Imani: *Or reliable.*

Another pause, longer this time.

Devon: *I like that.*

She read the message twice—not because of the words, but because of the tone.

Imani: *You like predictability?*

Devon: *I like knowing what I'm dealing with.*

Her fingers hovered before she responded. Then—

Imani: *That depends on how honest the situation is.*

She didn't soften it, didn't redirect or cushion the implication. She let it sit exactly where it landed.

Across the city, Devon leaned back in his chair, phone loose in his hand, rereading her message as the ghost of a smile tugged at his mouth—not amusement, but recognition.

"She's not letting that go," he murmured.

And he respected it, even as it complicated everything.

His apartment didn't match the image he projected; it wasn't unstable, but it wasn't settled either. Papers crowded the table, contracts sat half-signed, numbers moved faster than foundations.

He was building—but he had spoken like he'd already arrived. And Imani? She would see the difference.

He typed. Deleted. Typed again.

Devon: *You still thinking about that?*

Her reply took longer this time.

Imani: *I don't stop thinking. I categorize.*

He exhaled softly.

"That's worse," he said to no one.

Two days later, they met again—not by coincidence, but by choice.

The café was quieter than before, less curated and more honest, with wood tables and natural light and conversations that existed without performance.

Imani arrived first, as intended. This time, she didn't analyze the room or map exits; she allowed herself to occupy the space, because this wasn't a first impression but a continuation.

Devon entered minutes later, his gaze finding her immediately, and something about his posture shifted as he approached—not guarded, but more aware.

He sat across from her.

"You chose this place."

"I did."

"Why?"

She gestured lightly around them.

"Less controlled," she said. *"Easier to see people clearly."*

A corner of his mouth lifted.

"Is that what you're doing?"

"Always."

The conversation resumed without warm-up, work still present but deeper now, focused on process instead of presentation.

"What's your biggest challenge right now?" he asked evenly.

Devon hesitated, because this required a decision—image or truth.

"Scaling."

Safe.

She nodded. *"In what way?"*

Not safe.

He leaned back, tapping once against the table.

"Balancing growth with stability."

She waited. *"Meaning?"*

He exhaled, adjusting his words with care.

"Things are moving fast," he said, *"but not everything is as structured as I want it to be."*

True. Incomplete—but truthful enough to register.

"And that doesn't bother you?"

"It does."

"Then why frame it like it doesn't?"

There it was.

Devon met her gaze fully this time.

"Because people respond to confidence."

She nodded once.

"They do."

A pause, then—

"But I respond to truth."

The space between them cleared. Silence followed—not awkward, but clarifying.

Devon leaned forward slightly.

"What do you want me to say?"

She didn't hesitate.

"Exactly what you'd say if you weren't trying to impress me."

Another pause, then he smiled—not the polished version, but something quieter and more exposed.

"I'm not where I said I was."

There it was—no framing, no edge, just honesty.

She nodded.

"Okay."

He blinked.

"That's it?"

"What were you expecting?"

"A reaction."

Her lips curved faintly.

"That was it."

Something eased in his shoulders.

"Most people don't handle that well."

She tilted her head.

"Most people don't ask the questions I ask."

Fair. Undeniably so.

Later, they stepped outside as the city settled into itself. Devon stood slightly closer than before—not encroaching, not distant.

"I should've said it the first time."

"Why didn't you?"

He breathed in slowly.

"Because I wanted to be... enough."

That reached further than she expected, and her voice softened.

"You are."

A beat.

"But not like that."

He nodded.

"I know."

They stood there a moment longer, awareness replacing uncertainty.

"You're still evaluating me," he said.

"Yes."

"Fair."

Then—

"Just don't take too long."

"Why?"

A faint curve touched his mouth.

"Because I don't plan on staying exactly where I am."

She studied him, then—

"Good."

As Imani walked away, her thoughts didn't spiral, because now she had something usable—not perfect, not finished, but honest enough to build on.

Devon watched her go as something unfamiliar settled in his chest; he wasn't managing perception. He was standing in truth.

And unexpectedly—that felt better.

Chapter Ten: Not Supposed to Call

Nia Jackson did not check messages she wasn't expecting.

She especially didn't check messages she'd already decided not to receive, because expectation created access, and access created obligation—two things she guarded against instinctively.

Her phone lay face down on the counter while she moved through her apartment, the quiet of early evening settling around her like armor.

The space was clean, reset, controlled; she had showered, changed, restored order the way she always did after a shift, after a night, after anything that threatened to linger beyond permission.

Routine was her boundary.

Routine was her exit.

And whatever had happened on that rooftop—whatever had followed her somewhere she didn't revisit—had already been assigned its place.

Closed, finished, done—the internal punctuation she used when something no longer required attention.

Her phone buzzed.

She ignored it, pouring a drink and leaning against the counter while silence reclaimed the room, and she let her gaze drift without landing anywhere long enough to invite thought.

The phone buzzed again—longer this time, deliberate.

Nia's jaw tightened. That wasn't accidental. That was intentional.

She turned her head toward the phone like it had broken a rule she hadn't spoken aloud but fully expected to be respected.

"No," she said quietly, and the buzzing stopped.

Silence returned. She exhaled. Then—

The phone rang.

Nia froze, just for a second, before setting the glass down, because now this wasn't a possibility—it was a choice.

She picked up the phone. Unknown number.

She let it ring once more, then answered.

"Hello."

Calm. Even. Closed. A pause on the line. Then—

"You don't answer messages."

Jordan.

It was Jordan.

She closed her eyes briefly, recalibrating before responding.

"You weren't supposed to send one."

"You didn't say that."

"I didn't have to."

A pause followed—aware, undeniable.

"You left."

"Yes."

"Without a name."

"That was the point."

Another pause. Then—

"It didn't feel like the point."

There it was—the opening she didn't allow.

She leaned back against the counter, her gaze distant. *"It was. For me."*

"And for me?"

A quiet breath left her. *"You don't know me well enough for that to matter."*

The silence held, not dropped but considered.

"That's not how it felt."

Her grip tightened around the phone. *"That's exactly what it was."*

"Then why'd you answer?"

That irritated her, because the answer was simple, because the answer was right.

"To make sure you didn't keep calling."

"I was going to."

She expected that. *"You shouldn't have."*

"And you shouldn't have stayed."

Her eyes narrowed. *"That's not the same thing."*

"It is when it means something."

She pushed off the counter and paced slowly, the movement grounding her. *"It didn't mean anything."*

A longer pause followed. Then—

"You don't believe that."

She stopped, then moved again. *"Not your decision."*

"It is when I was there."

Her jaw set. *"You were there for a night."*

"You stayed longer than a night."

True.

Unwanted.

"That doesn't change anything."

"It changes enough."

She moved to the window, city lights pressing against the glass in quiet order—predictable in ways people weren't, steady in ways connection never seemed to be.

"Why are you calling me?"

Not sharp. Not soft. Clear.

"Because I wanted to hear your voice again."

Her breath shifted just enough that she noticed.

"That's not a reason."

"It is for me."

She shook her head. *"You don't even know my name."*

A pause. Then—

"Nia."

She went still. *"How—"*

"You left your badge in my kitchen."

"That doesn't mean you call me."

"It means I knew you weren't coming back for it."

—accurate, impossible to ignore, and suddenly the distance she'd assigned between them shifted. It had weight now.

"I can come get it."

Practical. Contained.

"You can."

A pause. Then—

"Or I can bring it to you."

Her reflection met her gaze in the glass. *"That's not necessary."*

"Neither was calling."

Quiet. Persistent. Unmoving. She turned from the window, pacing again.

"You're making this more than it is."

"Or you're making it less."

She stopped—because that struck.

Silence settled, not forced but present.

"What do you want?"

This time her voice held clarity, not resistance.

Jordan didn't rush.

"I want to see you again."

Her mind ran through every rule she'd written for herself—every boundary, every exit—and still, she didn't say no.

"That's not what we agreed to."

"We didn't agree to anything."

True.

She tightened her grip, then released it.

"Tomorrow."

The word escaped before control caught up.

A pause. Then—

"Tomorrow."

She closed her eyes, not in regret and not in panic. She stayed where she was.

The rules didn't disappear—but she didn't reach for them either.

The ending didn't feel clean.

It felt open.

Chapter Eleven: Professional Boundaries Blur

Zaria Bennett believed in boundaries—not loose ones, not flexible ones, but boundaries that were defined, structured, and maintained, especially in business.

Because once lines blurred in professional spaces, clarity disappeared, and Zaria didn't operate well in confusion.

Which was why, as she sat across from Malik at the long conference table hours after everyone else had left, her tablet lit with timelines and revisions while his laptop hummed softly between them, she was acutely aware that something about this situation no longer felt entirely… structured.

It wasn't the work.

The work was clear—refinement of the system, adjustments to flow, finalizing integration points before the next major event. All necessary. All expected.

What wasn't expected—.was how easily the hours had passed without either of them noticing the shift.

"I told you the delay was coming from the queue overload," Malik said, his voice calm and steady, not raised even slightly as he adjusted a line of code on his screen, its reflection casting faint light across his face.

Zaria didn't look up immediately. She finished reviewing the document in front of her, marked a note with precise efficiency, then finally leaned back, her gaze lifting toward him with measured acknowledgment.

"You told me after it happened," she replied.

"I told you while it was happening," he corrected.

She tilted her head slightly. *"That's not helpful in hindsight."*

"It's helpful in real time."

Zaria exhaled softly, a small sound of controlled irritation that didn't quite land as frustration.

"You don't let things go, do you?" she asked.

Malik's fingers paused over the keyboard for just a moment before continuing.

"Not when they're still relevant."

Zaria watched him a second longer than necessary, because that—that wasn't just about work.

And she knew it.

The room was quieter than it should have been—not empty, not uncomfortable, just contained, the kind of quiet that didn't push conversation but allowed it to surface naturally if it wanted to.

Zaria shifted in her seat, crossing one leg over the other as her tablet rested lightly against her thigh, her focus drifting not away from the work but around it.

"You stay late a lot?" she asked, her tone casual but intentional.

Malik didn't look up. *"When it matters."*

"That's vague."

"It's accurate."

She almost smiled.

Almost.

A beat passed. Then another. Then—

"You always work like this?" he asked, his voice cutting through the quiet without force.

Zaria's gaze lifted slightly. *"Like what?"*

"Like everything depends on it."

She leaned back slowly, her fingers tapping once against the edge of her tablet before stilling.

"Everything does," she replied.

This time, Malik glanced at her—really glanced—not a passing look or surface observation, but something more deliberate.

"That's not true," he said.

Zaria's brow lifted. *"It is when you're responsible for the outcome."*

"No," he said calmly. *"It's true when you decide it is."*

That—

that shifted something, subtle but real.

Zaria held his gaze, her expression composed, but something behind it adjusting slightly, like a recalibration she hadn't planned to make.

"You don't take responsibility seriously," she said.

Malik leaned back in his chair, finally closing his laptop halfway, his attention fully on her now.

"I take it exactly as seriously as it needs to be taken," he replied.

"And what does that mean?"

"It means I don't carry things that aren't mine to carry."

Zaria stared at him, because that—
that sounded like freedom.

And she didn't trust it.

"Must be nice," she said quietly.

Malik didn't answer right away. He didn't challenge it, just let the words sit for a moment before responding.

"It is."

Zaria let out a small breath, softer than her usual tone, less controlled.

"Yeah," she said, almost to herself. *"I imagine it is."*

The energy shifted again—not dramatically, but enough.

She stood and moved toward the window, her heels quiet against the floor, her reflection catching faintly in the glass as the city stretched out beyond her, alive and constant in a way that matched her internal rhythm more than she cared to admit.

"You know," she said, her voice softer now, less sharp, *"most people don't push back the way you do."*

Malik watched her from where he sat, his posture relaxed but attentive.

"Most people don't need to," he replied.

Zaria turned her head just enough to glance at him over her shoulder. *"And I do?"*

He held her gaze. *"Yes."*

No hesitation. No apology. Just truth.

She turned back to the window, her arms folding loosely across her chest as she processed that—not defensively, not emotionally, but thoughtfully.

"Why?" she asked.

Malik stood then, the movement quiet but noticeable, taking a few steps closer—not invading her space, not distant either.

"Because you don't leave space for anything else," he said.

Zaria didn't respond right away, because that—wasn't entirely wrong.

"I get results," she said instead.

He nodded. *"You do."*

A pause. Then—

"But at what cost?" he added.

Zaria's jaw tightened slightly. *"That's not your concern."*

"It is when I'm part of the outcome."

She turned fully then, facing him now, closer than before—not intentional, not avoided either.

"You're not part of my process," she said.

Malik met her where she stood, his tone steady, his expression unchanged.

"I'm part of the result."

That—

that was a line.

And Zaria felt it.

The space between them held, charged but not chaotic, focused.

"You're difficult," she said again, though this time the edge wasn't as sharp.

His mouth curved slightly. *"So are you."*

She let out a small breath that almost resembled a laugh.

"Yeah," she admitted quietly. *"I am."*

Another pause—closer now, different now.

"You didn't replace the blouse," she said suddenly, her tone shifting just enough to break the intensity.

Malik blinked once. Then—

"I said I would."

"You didn't."

"I didn't get the size."

Zaria raised an eyebrow slightly. *"You could've asked."*

"I could've," he agreed.

A beat. Then—

"Or you could tell me now."

There it was—that shift again, not professional, not entirely.

Zaria held his gaze, her lips pressing together briefly as she considered it, not the question itself but the ease of it, the way it moved past structure into something more natural.

"Medium," she said.

Malik nodded once. *"Got it."*

She didn't move away. Neither did he.

And for a moment—just a moment—the work didn't matter, the structure didn't matter, and the boundaries didn't feel as solid as they had before.

Then Zaria stepped back—not abruptly, not defensively, just intentionally.

"We should finish," she said, her tone returning to something more familiar.

Malik nodded. *"Yeah."*

They returned to the table, to the screens, to the work.

But something had shifted—quietly, irreversibly.

Because once boundaries blurred, even slightly, they didn't always return to where they were.

Chapter Twelve: The Almost Kiss

Maya didn't plan the third meeting.

That was the first thing she noticed.

The second was that she didn't question it.

It wasn't scheduled, didn't belong to anything she had organized or labeled.

It slipped into an in-between space—one of those stretches of time where routine loosened its grip just long enough for something unaccounted for to happen.

By the time she registered the shift, she had already said yes.

Now she stood outside his building, phone in hand, the city reflected faintly in the glass behind her.

The message remained on the screen.

Andre: *I'm home. Come up if you want.*

She didn't respond.

Instead, she slipped her phone into her bag, because answering would invite thought, and thought would lead to leaving.

She moved before either could catch up and stepped inside.

Andre opened the door before she knocked.

Not waiting—just present.

"You made it."

She walked past him without hesitation.

"Clearly."

The door closed softly behind her, sealing off the hallway noise.

His apartment was quiet—clean lines, minimal furniture, nothing excess or performative.

She scanned the room automatically.

"You don't decorate," she said, fingers brushing the back of a chair as she passed.

"I don't keep what I don't need."

She glanced back over her shoulder.

"That sounds philosophical."

"It's practical."

She hummed once, gaze drifting toward the windows where the city stretched out in muted light.

"It's also controlled."

Andre didn't respond.

He moved toward the kitchen, retrieved two glasses without asking what she wanted, and set one on the counter.

"Water?"

"Water's fine."

She joined him, her steps slower now, her posture less guarded without fully relaxing.

They remained standing.

No chairs pulled out.

No invitation to settle.

Close enough to register.

Far enough to resist.

"So," she said, fingers wrapping around the glass, *"what is this?"*

Andre leaned back slightly.

"You came over."

She exhaled.

"That's not an answer."

"It's accurate."

A quiet laugh escaped her before she could stop it.

"You're difficult."

"You've said that."

"Because it keeps proving itself."

He nodded once.

"Consistency matters to you."

She met his gaze.

"It does."

Silence settled—not heavy, just attentive.

After a moment—

"You didn't ask why I came," she said.

"If it matters," he replied, *"you'll tell me."*

Most people filled space. Andre didn't.

Against her better judgment, she spoke.

"I don't do this."

He stayed still, listening.

"I don't walk into things without knowing the outcome," she continued. *"I don't leave situations undefined. I don't—"*

She stopped, then finished quietly.

"—improvise."

"I know."

She blinked.

"You do?"

"You've shown me."

Her grip tightened briefly around the glass, then loosened.

"And yet," she said, softer now, *"here I am."*

A faint curve touched his mouth.

"Here you are."

The air changed—not movement, not sound.

Awareness.

She set the glass down carefully and took one small step closer.

Not enough to touch.

Enough to matter.

"You don't make this easy."

Andre didn't move.

"I'm not trying to."

She searched his face—for leverage, for reaction.

Found neither.

"That's the problem."

"It doesn't have to be."

"It is for me."

A pause.

"Why?"

Her gaze dropped, then lifted.

"Because I don't know what to do with this."

Andre watched her without reframing it.

"You don't have to do anything."

She shook her head once.

"That's not how I work."

"I know."

She frowned.

"Then why say that?"

"Because not everything needs managing."

The space between them tightened.

She stepped closer—deliberate this time.

"You keep doing that."

"Doing what?"

"Making complicated things sound simple."

"Because sometimes they are."

"No."

"They are," he said. *"You just don't trust that."*

Her breath shifted.

"You don't know that."

"I do."

For a moment, everything aligned—the stillness, the space, the quiet pull forward.

Her eyes dipped to his mouth. Returned to his eyes.

And she stopped.

Andre didn't move. Didn't close the distance she let hang between them. That restraint unsettled her more than pursuit would have.

She stepped back abruptly, tension snapping back into place.

"I shouldn't be here."

Her voice steadied as control slid back into position.

"If that's how you feel."

She turned sharply.

"You're not going to stop me?"

"No."

"Why not?"

"Because you're not leaving for the reason you're saying."

That landed too close.

"You don't get to decide that."

"I'm not deciding," he said. *"I'm noticing."*

She grabbed her bag.

"You're exhausting."

"And you're still here."

She froze for half a second.

Then—

"I'm leaving."

Andre didn't follow her. Didn't reach.

She opened the door and paused, hand resting against it while her breath slowed and her thoughts didn't. Then she stepped into the hall and closed the door softly behind her.

The moment stayed unfinished.

Inside, Andre remained where she'd left him, eyes on the door long after it closed.

Outside, Maya's heels struck the pavement faster than necessary. She didn't slow. Didn't look back.

And for once—she didn't name it.

Chapter Thirteen: Screenshots & Suspicions

The group chat didn't just talk—it investigated, dissected, and cross-referenced, because when something didn't sit right it didn't stay private; it was pulled into the space where humor softened sharp truth just enough to make it survivable.

Imani didn't usually bring uncertainty into the chat, not like this and not unfinished, but tonight, seated at her dining table with her laptop open and untouched and her tea gone cold beside her, she stared at her phone longer than usual before typing—because this wasn't a feeling.

It was a pattern.

And patterns required confirmation.

She finally typed.

Imani: *I need objective opinions.*

alone shifted everything.

Maya: *Oh. It's serious.*

Zaria: *Very serious. She said "objective."*

Nia: *I'm here.*

Imani exhaled slowly.

Imani: *I'm sending screenshots.*

A pause followed. Then—

Nia: *Okay yeah, this is about to be good.*

Maya: *Send them.*

Zaria: *Immediately.*

The first screenshot appeared.

A clean thread. Polished words. Controlled cadence. Nothing overtly wrong—but wrong all the same.

Devon: *Long day. Back to back meetings.*

Maya: *What time was this?*

Imani: *3:12 PM.*

Another screenshot followed, timestamped earlier.

Devon: *Just finished building a new system. Had to get hands on today.*

Silence struck the chat.

Then—

Maya: *...okay.*

Nia: *Yeah, no.*

Zaria: *Those don't coexist.*

Imani felt confirmation, not satisfaction.

Imani: *Exactly.*

Maya: *You can't be in meetings and hands on development at the same time.*

Nia: *Unless you're exaggerating.*

Zaria: *Or lying.*

Imani didn't answer yet. She had more.

Another screenshot.

Devon: *We're expanding fast. Signed multiple new clients.*

Then another.

Devon: *Trying to keep things stable while I build the client base.*

The responses were immediate.

Maya: *Oh.*

Nia: *Mm no.*

Zaria: *That's early stage, not expansion.*

Imani leaned back, her fingers resting against the table.

Imani: *He admitted he's not where he said he was.*

That shifted the tone.

Maya: *Okay. So he told the truth eventually.*

Nia: *That matters.*

Zaria: *It does. But why not upfront?*

Imani scanned the messages, because that was the question.

Imani: *He said he wanted to be enough.*

The chat stilled—not confusion, but recognition.

Maya: *That's honest… but it's also a problem.*

Nia: *Because he builds perception first.*

Zaria: *Which means you'll always double-check him.*

Imani nodded to herself.

Imani: *That's what I'm deciding.*

Maya's response came quickly.

Maya: *Do you like him?*

Imani stared at the screen, because liking him complicated the math.

Imani: *Yes.*

Simple. Unavoidable.

Nia: *Okay. So the question isn't whether he's flawed.*

Zaria: *Because he is.*

Maya: *Obviously.*

Nia: *The question is whether his flaw is manageable.*

Imani inhaled slowly.

Imani: *I don't tolerate inconsistency.*

Maya: *You never have.*

Zaria: *Not even a little.*

Nia: *So can you tolerate his version?*

Imani closed her eyes briefly.

He's not inconsistent, she thought. *He's strategic.*

She typed.

Imani: *He controls what he reveals.*

The replies came fast.

Maya: *That's not better.*

Nia: *That's calculated.*

Zaria: *And dangerous.*

Imani sat with that, because danger wasn't always loud.

Sometimes it was smooth, measured, well-presented.

Another message appeared.

Maya: *Describe the way he looks at you.*

Imani frowned.

Imani: *That's not quantifiable.*

Maya: *It is emotionally.*

Nia: *Same.*

Zaria: *Yeah, drop the analysis—give us the data point.*

Imani exhaled, then answered.

Imani: *Like he wants to be seen… but isn't convinced it's safe.*

The chat stalled—longer this time.

Maya: *Okay. That's different.*

Nia: *That's not manipulation.*

Zaria: *That's insecurity.*

Imani nodded.

Yes.

Maya: *So now the real question—*

Nia: *Does he grow?*

Zaria: *Or do you end up managing him?*

Imani's response didn't hesitate.

Imani: *I don't manage people.*

The answers came instantly.

Maya: *No, you don't.*

Nia: *Never have.*

Zaria: *Never will.*

Imani felt alignment settle in her chest.

Imani: *So if he stays where he is…*

Maya: *You walk.*

Nia: *Immediately.*

Zaria: *No exceptions.*

She nodded once.

But—

Imani: *If he doesn't...*

A pause followed. Then—

Maya: *Then you stay.*

Nia: *And observe.*

Zaria: *Carefully.*

Imani lowered her phone, because this wasn't uncertainty anymore—it was a decision.

Across the city, Devon sat alone, his phone in his hand as he stared at a message unsent, clarity cutting clean.

Imani Clarke was not someone he could present a version of himself to.

He would show up real—Or not at all.

Chapter Fourteen: Unexpected Depth

Nia Jackson didn't prepare for second meetings.

First ones were easy—contained, defined, temporary, with built-in exits and no obligation, no evolution, and no reason to remember anything beyond the moment itself.

Second meetings required intention.

And intention required acknowledgment.

She stood in front of the mirror longer than necessary, hands resting at her sides, her gaze steady but unsettled. The outfit was simple—she didn't do complicated—but she'd changed twice, which told her more than she wanted to know.

"This is unnecessary," she murmured.

She didn't move.

Not yet, because moving would make the decision real.

Jordan didn't text when he arrived.

He called—again.

Her phone lit, and something tightened just behind her ribs as she answered before it could ring long enough to feel like a choice.

"Hello."

"I'm outside."

No preamble, no buffer, just presence.

"I'll be down."

She was already reaching for the door.

The evening air held that quiet pause between day and night as Nia stepped onto the sidewalk and saw him immediately—same stillness, same grounded calm, the same way he occupied space without claiming it.

"You came," he said.

"I said I would."

He nodded once.

"You did."

They didn't go to his place, and that was the first difference.

They walked instead, no plan and no destination, just movement—side by side, not touching but not distant either, intentional without being declared.

After a few blocks, he spoke.

"You left something."

"I know."

"You weren't coming back for it."

She exhaled.

"No."

"I figured."

A pause.

"Why'd you keep it?" she asked.

He didn't answer right away.

"Because I knew I'd see you again."

That wasn't confidence.

That was certainty.

And she didn't trust certainty.

"That's not how this works."

"How does it work?"

"It doesn't."

He nodded.

"That's what you tell yourself."

She stopped walking. He took one more step, then stopped too.

"That's what I know."

He met her gaze.

"Then why are you here?"

There it was—again, simple and unavoidable.

She didn't have a clean answer, not one she liked.

"I came for my badge."

The faintest curve touched his mouth.

"That's not why you stayed."

"Everything doesn't have to mean something."

"It doesn't," he said calmly. *"But this does."*

The city moved around them—cars passing, voices overlapping, life continuing—but Nia felt the stillness settle, the weight, the shift refusing to be ignored.

"You don't know me," she said, softer now.

Jordan stepped closer, not encroaching—just present.

"Then let me."

That was the problem, because letting him meant opening something, and opening something meant risk.

She looked away, scanning streetlights and passing faces, anything to anchor herself back to certainty.

"I don't stay."

"I didn't ask you to."

She turned back to him.

"You are."

"I'm asking you to stop running before there's something to run from."

Silence fell, and it struck deeper than she wanted it to, because it wasn't wrong.

"You don't get to decide that."

"I'm not deciding," he replied. *"I'm noticing."*

Her shoulders dropped a fraction.

"You notice too much."

He shrugged.

"You leave too fast."

That almost pulled a smile from her—almost.

They started walking again, slower now, closer.

"You don't ask many questions," she said.

"Only the important ones."

"Then ask one."

He looked at her.

"What are you afraid of?"

She stopped, because that wasn't casual and wasn't surface.

She met his eyes.

"That this becomes something."

No filter. No deflection.

"That's not a bad thing."

"It is when it doesn't last."

A pause.

"Nothing lasts forever," he said. *"That doesn't make it meaningless."*

Her breath slowed.

"You make it sound simple."

"It is."

"No," she said quietly. *"It's not."*

He stepped closer—closer than before.

"It doesn't have to be complicated unless you make it that way."

Something shifted then, not just between them, but within her, because this wasn't supposed to feel like anything—and it did.

She stepped closer, not calculating, not negotiating, just responding.

Their hands brushed, light and intentional, acknowledged without hesitation. She didn't pull away.

"Tomorrow was a mistake," she said softly.

He shook his head.

"No," he replied. *"It wasn't."*

She looked at him, unguarded but not unprotected.

"That's what makes it dangerous."

His hand closed around hers, not possessive—present.

"Or worth it."

She didn't answer, because she didn't have one.

And that changed everything.

Chapter Fifteen: The Event Disaster

Zaria Barrett didn't believe in failure—not because failure didn't happen, but because she never allowed it to finish.

There was always a pivot, a correction, a way to force momentum back into alignment before anyone important noticed the cracks, and that discipline was her reputation, her standard, and what tonight was meant to confirm.

The venue exceeded her usual scale—multi-level, high-profile, the kind of event where presentation mattered as much as performance.

Screens wrapped the walls, lighting pulsed in precise sequences, and the guest list—the guest list mattered enough to dictate everything that followed.

Investors. Founders. Decision-makers. People who remembered disruption long after the room emptied.

Zaria moved through the space like ownership was implied, tablet in hand, attention split across timing cues, staff placement, flow patterns, and system response, her heels striking the floor with exact rhythm. Everything was in place, everything aligned—

"Zaria."

She didn't stop.

"What?"

"The system's lagging again."

Her stride slowed, then stopped entirely.

"Where?"

"Check-in and live display."

Her jaw tightened.

"Fix it."

"We're trying—"

"No," she cut in evenly. *"Don't try. Fix it."*

Across the room, Malik noticed the shift before he saw it, because the energy didn't spike—it skewed, the kind of disruption that began subtly before spreading.

He closed his laptop, scanning the screens as they fell out of rhythm.

"Queue's stacking," he murmured, already standing.

Zaria reached the check-in station just as the line slowed—not stalled, but tight enough to generate friction as guests shifted weight and glances sharpened.

"What's happening?"

"Same issue," a staff member replied.

Updates aren't processing fast enough."

"That's not possible," Zaria said. *"We fixed this."*

"We thought we did."

Unacceptable.

"Move people manually," she ordered. *"Split the line. Override. Keep it moving."*

The staff moved quickly, but Zaria didn't, because it would hold—for now.

"Where's Malik?"

She hadn't meant to ask.

That irritated her.

"Here."

His voice came from behind her—calm, unrushed—and when she turned, he was already there. He wasn't panicking.

"It's not holding," she said.

"I know."

"Then fix it."

"I am."

He stepped past her, setting his laptop down as his fingers moved with immediate focus. Zaria gave him space—not because she wanted to, but because she understood efficiency.

"What changed?"

"Live update about an hour ago."

Malik nodded. *"That's the failure point."*

"It wasn't earlier."

"It is now."

She scanned the room. Five minutes would be noticed.

"How long?"

"Five."

Too long.

"Make it three."

He paused, then looked up. *"Not how this works."*

She met his gaze. *"It is tonight."*

A beat.

"Four," he said.

"Done."

The next four minutes stretched and compressed all at once as Zaria moved constantly—redirecting staff, smoothing guest interactions, controlling optics—while her attention kept returning to Malik, the way he didn't rush, didn't react, didn't bend under pressure.

"Now."

The screens stabilized, the lag disappeared, and flow resumed.

Zaria inhaled—not visibly, but deeply.

"It'll hold," Malik said, closing his laptop.

She looked at him not as a complication, but as a solution.

"Thank you."

Clean.

Direct.

Unqualified.

"You're welcome."

The event recovered, energy returning to rhythm as guests relaxed and everything looked exactly as planned. Zaria stayed where she was, watching the system run.

"You trust me now?" Malik asked.

She glanced at him. *"I trust outcomes."*

His mouth curved faintly. *"Fair."*

A pause.

"You stayed," she said.

"I said I would."

That mattered more than she wanted it to.

Later, as the event wound down and the room softened, Malik approached again.

"You handled that well."

Zaria exhaled. *"I had help."*

"You had control."

She met his gaze. *"Not the whole time."*

The admission surprised her.

"You don't always have to," he said quietly.

She absorbed that.

"Yeah," she said. *"Maybe."*

The space between them shifted—closer now, different.

"You still owe me a blouse," she said lightly.

"I didn't forget."

She stepped closer, not planned and not avoided.

"Good."

This time, the tension wasn't conflict.

It was possibility.

Something beginning.

Something neither of them was pretending not to see.

Chapter Sixteen: The Truth Leak

Imani Clarke did not like surprises—not the public kind, not the kind that confirmed instincts she hadn't yet been ready to name, because she preferred information before impact, clarity before confrontation, and control before visibility.

Which was why, as she stepped into the networking lounge—an extension of the same professional orbit they'd all begun inhabiting—she was already reading the room.

The space was polished without stiffness, conversations layered in low tones, introductions masked as casual exchanges, the kind of environment where reputations circulated quietly and were validated or dismantled without ceremony.

Imani moved with ease—not guarded or performative, just precise in the way she always was when observation mattered more than engagement.

She saw Devon before he saw her.

Across the room, surrounded by a cluster that carried weight—not loudly, but unmistakably—he stood at ease, posture confident and cadence practiced, and for a moment he looked exactly like the version he'd presented.

Imani approached without signaling, not to catch him off balance, but because context mattered more than advantage.

"...scaling too fast without stability is where people slip," someone remarked thoughtfully.

Devon nodded.

"Agreed," he said smoothly. *"That's why we've stayed selective."*

Selective.

That word again.

Imani noted it.

"And how many clients are you managing right now?" another voice asked.

There it was, clean and simple and unavoidable.

Devon didn't hesitate.

"Enough to stay in demand."

Imani felt it immediately—the same phrasing, the same positioning.

"And your team?" someone pressed.

"Expanding," Devon replied. *"Keeping it lean."*

Imani stepped closer, not abruptly but decisively, and Devon's eyes flicked toward her for a fraction of a second before returning to the group—but she saw it.

"Imani," he said easily. *"Good to see you."*

She nodded. *"Devon."*

"You two know each other?" someone asked.

"Yes," Imani replied, and said nothing more.

"Perfect," the same man said lightly. *"Maybe you can clarify something for us."*

Not an attack. A setup.

"You mentioned selectivity, but also growth," he continued. *"Which stage would you say you're actually in?"*

Silence followed—focused, expectant.

Devon's posture held and his expression stayed neutral, but something behind it tightened just enough to be noticeable if you were paying attention.

Imani watched him, not to expose and not to protect, but to see.

"Growth," Devon said again.

Same answer. Same deflection.

Imani stepped forward, not dramatically but intentionally.

"Early growth," she said.

The room shifted—just slightly.

Devon turned fully this time, and Imani met his gaze, calm and accurate as she continued.

"Stabilizing infrastructure while building consistency," she added evenly. *"It's transitional."*

Truth settled without resistance. Heads nodded.

"That makes sense."

"More sustainable."

"Smarter."

The tension dissolved, because clarity did that.

Devon nodded.

"Exactly."

And this time it didn't sound rehearsed.

The conversation moved on without spectacle, and minutes later the cluster dispersed, leaving space and quiet—and them.

Neither spoke immediately. They stood side by side, no longer uncertain, just exposed.

"You didn't have to do that," Devon said at last.

"I didn't do it for you," Imani replied, honest as always.

He nodded. *"I know."*

Then—*"But you didn't let it collapse."*

"I don't let situations misrepresent themselves," she said.

Devon exhaled, not frustration and not relief, but something suspended between the two.

"I was going to correct it."

She looked at him.

"When?"

That was the moment.

He paused, because no clean answer existed.

"Before it mattered."

"It already did."

Silence held—real this time.

"You see everything," he said, not admiration and not complaint, just recognition.

"I pay attention."

He looked at her longer now, less guarded, and when he spoke again his voice held something stripped back.

"I don't want to keep doing that."

"Doing what?"

"Managing perception instead of owning reality."

That mattered.

"Then don't," she replied simply.

He nodded. *"Okay."*

Then—*"You might not like what that looks like."*

She didn't flinch.

"I don't need to like it," she said. *"I need to trust it."*

That landed, and Devon's shoulders eased.

"Okay."

This time it wasn't filler.

It was choice.

Around them, the room continued, unaware, but for Imani the guessing was over. The only question left was whether he would follow through.

And for Devon, there was no longer anywhere to hide—only space to show up.

Or walk away.

Chapter Seventeen: Distance & Doubt

Maya Reynolds did not revisit moments she couldn't control.

She filed them, labeled them, and moved on—not because they didn't matter, but because naming them too precisely gave them weight she couldn't always manage.

Structure kept things clean. Distance kept them quiet.

Three days after standing in Andre's apartment—after stepping into something she hadn't defined and stepping out before it could define her—she did what she always did when something slipped outside containment.

She pulled back.

Clean.

Intentional.

Efficient.

Or at least that was the idea.

Her phone rested beside her laptop as she worked, the screen filled with design frameworks and user pathways.

Logic grounded her the way it always did.

Inputs.

Outputs.

Predictable responses.

People didn't work like that.

Andre didn't.

The first day, she didn't text him.

The second day, she noticed the impulse and ignored it.

By the third, she told herself there was nothing to respond to—because he hadn't reached out either.

That part surprised her more than she expected.

No call.

No message.

No attempt to bridge the space she'd created.

Maya leaned back slightly in her chair.

"You're not going to chase," she murmured.

Her phone buzzed.

She didn't reach for it right away.

If it was him, it would matter.

If it wasn't, it wouldn't.

Either way, she picked it up.

Group Chat: Frequency

Zaria: *I'm tired.*

Nia: *That's new.*

Zaria: *Not physically. Mentally.*

Maya: *What happened now?*

Imani: *Let her talk.*

Maya set the phone down beside her keyboard, listening with half her attention.

Zaria: *The event went well... but something felt off.*

Nia: *Off how?*

Zaria: *Like I wasn't fully in control.*

Maya: *You hate that.*

Zaria: *I do.*

A pause followed.

Zaria: *But I didn't hate it as much as I thought I would.*

Maya's brow lifted before she caught it.

That was different.

Nia: *Oh, you're gone.*

Zaria: *I AM NOT GONE.*

Maya: *You're adjusting.*

Imani: *That's different.*

Another pause.

Zaria: *He stayed.*

Maya: *Malik?*

Zaria: *Yes.*

Nia: *Yeah… you're gone.*

Maya: *Completely.*

Zaria: *I hate all of you.*

Maya smiled faintly, but the reaction didn't fully land.

Imani: *How are you handling it?*

Zaria: *I don't know yet.*

That word again.

Yet.

Maya typed.

Maya: *You'll figure it out.*

The message read supportive. Casual.

Practiced.

It didn't feel detached.

The conversation carried on—Nia redirecting, Imani grounding, Zaria resisting—but Maya's attention drifted back to the same quiet space she'd been avoiding.

No contact.

No follow-up.

No retrieval.

She stood and moved to the window, arms folding loosely as the city shifted below her.

"Say something," she murmured—not to him, but to herself.

She wasn't used to this feeling.

Someone creating space without retreating.

Someone staying put when she stepped back.

Her phone vibrated again.

This time—a direct message.

Her breath shifted as she crossed the room.

Andre: *Hope your week's been productive.*

Maya stared at the screen longer than necessary.

Of course that was what he said.

Not *I miss you.*

Not *Where did you go.*

Not *Why haven't you reached out.*

Just—

Hope your week's been productive.

She let out a quiet breath, halfway between a laugh and disbelief.

"Aww," she said softly.

Her fingers moved.

Paused.

Deleted.

She typed again.

Maya: *It has been.*

Sent.

Short.

Neutral.

Contained.

The typing indicator appeared.

Disappeared.

Returned.

Her grip tightened slightly.

Andre: *Good.*

That was it.

No opening.

No reach.

No follow-up.

Just—

good.

Maya leaned back against the counter, phone loose in her hand.

"That's it?" she murmured.

Something settled low in her chest—not sharp, not painful. Just unfamiliar.

The distance wasn't only hers anymore.

Across the city, Andre set his phone down on the table, posture relaxed, expression unreadable.

He had checked in.

He had answered.

He left the rest where it belonged.

What Maya did next wasn't his to manage.

Back in her apartment, Maya stared at the thread again—not to reread it, not to decode it, but because she wasn't setting the pace.

And she didn't know yet whether that unsettled her—or steadied her.

Chapter Eighteen: The Line Crossed

Nia Jackson didn't do weekends—not the kind that stretched, not the kind that lingered, not the kind that blurred time into continuity. Her life moved in segments—shifts with purpose, work, rest, reset, repeat—and boundaries lived inside that rhythm the same way safety did.

So when Friday night slid unnoticed into Saturday morning, and Saturday refused to end, she knew before she questioned it—something had already crossed.

It started the way things always did: simply.

She told herself she would stop by, keep it short, keep it light, and maintain the distance she'd defined the first time she walked away.

Jordan opened the door as if expectation wasn't a calculation but a given—not because she'd said what time she'd arrive, but because she'd said she would.

"You came."

She stepped inside without hesitation, expression composed, though her eyes scanned the room differently this time, because now it wasn't new—and familiarity carried weight.

"You're early."

"I don't do late entrances."

He nodded once, closing the door behind her.

"Consistent."

"Don't analyze me."

"I'm not. I'm noticing."

She exhaled softly.

"Same thing."

"Not always."

They didn't rush or collapse into proximity, and that was the second difference, because the first time had been physical—immediate and contained—while this time there was space.

"Want something to drink?"

"Water's fine."

He moved into the kitchen and she followed without thinking, her steps slower and her presence less guarded, though not fully open.

"You working this weekend?"

"Not until Sunday night."

He nodded once.

"So you have time."

That wasn't a question.

Her grip tightened slightly around the glass as she leaned back against the counter.

"Time for what?"

He met her eyes without hesitation.

"To stay."

Silence followed—clear, plain, inescapable.

"Don't do that," she said quietly.

"Do what?"

"Make it sound simple."

"It is simple."

"No," she said, shaking her head. *"It isn't."*

He stepped closer, not forcefully or fast, just enough to register.

"It's only complicated if you make it that way."

She looked at him—really looked—and what she found wasn't pressure or persuasion or strategy; it was presence.

"I don't stay," she said again.

He nodded.

"I know."

That disarmed her more than any argument could have.

"Then why say it?"

"I didn't ask," he replied. *"I said you have time."*

She exhaled slowly, because the distinction mattered.

"Time doesn't mean availability."

"It means opportunity."

A pause settled between them.

She set the glass down, then stepped closer, because this wasn't something she could think her way through—not this time.

What followed wasn't rushed. It unfolded slower than before, deliberate, with every movement acknowledged, and somewhere between the first hour and the second and the third, time lost its structure entirely.

Saturday morning arrived quietly as light filtered in and the city rested.

Nia sat at the edge of the bed, fingers resting loosely against the fabric, listening to the shared quiet that didn't feel temporary.

"You're still here."

She didn't turn.

"I know."

A pause followed.

"You don't usually stay."

"No."

He moved closer, present without touching.

"Why now?"

That question required something she rarely gave.

"I don't know."

Unfiltered.

Uncomfortable.

True.

He didn't respond immediately—and he didn't need to, because that answer said enough.

Saturday bled into afternoon, afternoon into evening, as they left the apartment and walked, ate, talked—not about everything, but about enough.

She found herself speaking without rehearsing exits, staying in moments she'd normally abandon early, and Jordan didn't push or define or claim.

He stayed.

Sunday morning came quietly, and this time she felt it before opening her eyes—the shift, the weight, the difference.

She sat up slowly, awareness catching up to reality, because this wasn't casual anymore and it couldn't be.

"You're thinking."

She glanced at him.

"Yeah."

He waited, knowing she'd speak when ready.

"This is different."

He nodded.

"It is."

A pause followed.

"That's a problem."

He studied her.

"No," he said. *"It isn't."*

Her expression stayed steady even as her eyes did not.

"It is for me."

Because now there was something to lose, and that had never been part of the plan.

She stood and moved slowly.

"I should go."

He didn't argue or stop her.

"Okay."

That made it harder, because he wasn't holding her—she had to choose, and she wasn't ready.

Not yet.

She reached the door and paused, her hand resting against the handle.

Then—

"I'll see you again."

Not a question, not a promise, something in between.

He nodded once.

"You will."

And this time neither of them questioned it, because whatever they had crossed, they had crossed together.

And there was no going back.

Chapter Nineteen: Public Embarrassment

Imani Clarke did not embarrass easily. She didn't offer people access to that version of her—the unsettled one, the exposed one, the one caught mid-calculation with no adjustment ready—because she moved with too much intention for that and paid too close attention to how perception shaped reality in rooms where everyone pretended it didn't matter.

But embarrassment didn't always announce itself.

Sometimes—it arrived quietly.

Then settled in public.

The room carried weight—not loudness, but presence, conversations layered over one another while introductions circled back in familiar patterns and influence shifted subtly from one cluster to the next. This was where reputations were measured, not granted, and Imani measured back.

She stood near the center of the space, posture relaxed, expression composed, her attention sharp enough to register shifts others missed. Devon stood beside her, close enough to suggest alignment but not close enough to define it.

"You didn't say it would be this crowded," he murmured.

She didn't look at him right away. *"It's a networking event,"* she replied evenly. *"People tend to show up to those."*

He released a breath that almost counted as a laugh.

"Fair."

There was no overt tension, but there wasn't ease either, because now everything between them carried context—truth, exposure, expectation.

They moved together through the room, introductions made, conversations joined and released, until the rhythm pulled them apart—and then it didn't pull them back together.

Imani stepped into a conversation she hadn't initiated but didn't avoid, a small group that was observant and economical with attention. Devon joined a moment later, and that's when it shifted.

"You're the one behind the Harris Group, right?" a man asked, his tone casual but evaluative.

"That's me," Devon replied.

Imani felt it—the slight internal tightening she recognized immediately.

"Your name's been circulating," the man continued. *"Scaling fast. Multiple contracts. Impressive."*

Devon smiled, measured.

"I appreciate that."

Imani's gaze sharpened, because the phrasing was familiar—too familiar.

What sectors are you focused on right now?" another voice asked.

"Tech infrastructure. Consulting. Integration support," Devon answered.

Not wrong.

Not complete.

"And your team size?" the first man followed.

There it was again, clean and direct.

Devon paused—not long enough to be obvious, just long enough to be noticed.

"We're growing," he said.

Imani felt it clearly this time, that adjustment, that positioning.

"And currently?" the man pressed.

The room didn't quiet.

It focused.

Devon opened his mouth, then closed it.

"We're building capacity to support expansion."

Imani's stomach tightened, because that wasn't an answer—and this time, it didn't pass.

"So still early stage," the man said, not unkindly, just accurate.

Devon's expression held, didn't crack, but something shifted beneath it.

"We're positioning for growth."

Imani stepped back—not with her feet, but with her trust—because now this wasn't interpretation or subtle misalignment or a private space where truth could be calibrated without consequence.

This was public.

And he was still doing it.

The conversation moved on smoothly and politely, but perception had already adjusted, and Imani felt it—not for him, but for herself, because she was standing beside him while it happened, associated, present, part of a moment where clarity should have been easy and wasn't.

"Excuse me," she said quietly.

She didn't wait. She moved through the room, past conversations and glances, past the awareness that something had shifted, and stepped outside.

The air was cooler, sharper, real, and Imani Clarke felt something she didn't allow.

Embarrassment.

Not loud.

Not visible.

Internal. Immediate. Unavoidable.

She folded her arms loosely, steadying herself not emotionally but structurally, the way she always did when something violated alignment.

"You left."

voice reached her from behind. She didn't turn right away—then she did.

"Yes."

He stepped closer, not crowding, just present.

"You didn't have to do that."

Imani met his gaze, and this time there was no softening.

"I didn't have to stay either."

landed, and his shoulders tightened briefly.

"It wasn't that serious."

Her expression didn't change.

"It was to me."

Silence stretched, unbalanced.

"You're making it bigger than it is."

That—

that was the wrong thing to say.

Imani's posture sharpened.

No," she said quietly. *"I'm naming it accurately."*

He hesitated.

"I told you I wasn't where I said I was."

"You did."

A pause.

"But you're still presenting like you are."

That was the difference.

Devon ran a hand along his jaw.

"I'm not trying to mislead anyone."

She held his gaze.

"But you are."

Silence, because intent didn't matter—impact did.

"You stood next to me," she continued evenly, *"and continued something you already acknowledged wasn't accurate."*

His jaw tightened.

"I didn't correct it fast enough."

She shook her head once.

"You didn't correct it at all."

That was the truth, and it sat between them.

"I'm working on it."

She nodded slowly.

"Then work on it," she said.

A beat.

"But don't ask me to stand in it while you do."

That ended it.

Devon didn't argue. There was nothing left to reframe.

Imani turned—not abruptly, not emotionally, but decisively—and this time she didn't look back, because clarity didn't require repetition.

Chapter Twenty: You Should've Said Something

Imani Clarke did not call people in the middle of emotional moments. She waited until reactions settled into conclusions, until time had done enough work for clarity to emerge, because confrontation, to her, wasn't about release—it was about resolution.

So when she walked away from Devon that night, she didn't look back. And she didn't reach out.

Not until she understood exactly what needed to be said.

Her apartment felt quieter than usual—not empty, not cold, but reflective, the kind of quiet that didn't distract from thought so much as amplify it.

She set her bag down by the door, slipped out of her shoes, hung her blazer with care, and placed her phone face down on the table. Routine.

Except tonight, the routine didn't resolve anything.

She moved into the kitchen, poured water she didn't drink, and stood there too long while her mind replayed the moment—not emotionally and not dramatically, but clinically.

Word by word, tone by tone, choice for choice, every detail replayed with precision.

"It wasn't that serious."

Her jaw tightened, because that—that was the fracture.

She picked up her phone and turned it over. No messages.

She didn't wait for people to correct what they broke; she addressed it.

Her phone lit in her hand.

Devon: *We need to talk.*

Imani read it once, then again, not surprised and not persuaded.

She typed.

Imani: *Tomorrow.*

Sent.

Clear, bounded, final.

She set the phone down again. Tonight wasn't for conversation—it was for clarity.

The next day didn't rush; it unfolded deliberate and measured, and Imani chose the location.

Neutral ground, no advantage, no performance, no escape—nothing incidental, nothing uncontrolled.

When she arrived, Devon was already there, and that told her something.

She stepped inside minutes later, her posture composed and her presence exact.

He stood when he saw her.

"Imani."

She nodded. *"Devon."*

No embrace, no easing-in, no pretense of comfort that hadn't been earned.

They sat, and silence held—not because there was nothing to say, but because what needed saying required accuracy.

"You left," Devon said.

She met his gaze. *"Yes."*

A pause followed.

"I needed to."

He nodded once. *"I understand."*

She didn't respond, because understanding didn't resolve impact.

"I should have handled that differently," he said.

There it was.

She leaned back slightly, her hands resting in her lap. *"Yes."*

No cushioning, no softening—truth didn't require either.

He exhaled, his composure loosening.

"I didn't want to look like I didn't have it together."

Imani tilted her head. *"You didn't."*

Not harsh—accurate.

"I know," he said quietly.

A pause.

"But I didn't want you to see me like that."

Her expression didn't shift. *"You already knew I did."*

"That's different."

"How?"

"You saw it privately," he said. *"Last night was public."*

Imani leaned forward, her tone firm but level.

"Do you think my standard changes based on audience?"

He didn't answer immediately—because it didn't.

"No."

She nodded once. *"Then why would your behavior?"*

Silence answered first.

He ran a hand through his hair, restraint slipping. *"I thought I could manage it."*

Imani held her ground. *"That's the problem."*

A pause.

"You shouldn't have to manage the truth."

That struck deeper.

He leaned back, his posture no longer curated. *"I've been doing that for a long time."*

"I can tell."

"And it's worked."

She tilted her head again. *"Has it?"*

Because success wasn't sustainability.

He hesitated. *"It got me here."*

She leaned back. *"Where is here?"*

That forced it.

He exhaled slowly. *"Still building."*

She nodded. *"That's fine."*

Then—

"But say that."

Simple and direct, without framing or defense.

"You should've said something," she continued, not angry and not disappointed—expectant.

He looked at her, really looked.

"I thought I was."

She shook her head once. *"No. You were managing perception."*

That distinction was everything.

"And I don't do that," she added.

He nodded. *"I know."*

Silence returned—not tense and not unresolved, just real.

"So what happens now?" he asked.

Imani didn't hesitate. *"That depends on you."*

A pause.

"I don't lower my standard," she said, her tone steady and her eyes clear.

"But I do allow growth."

That was the space—not forgiveness, not assurance, but opportunity.

Devon leaned forward, his expression stripped of polish.

"I'm not going to keep doing that."

Imani met his gaze. *"Then don't."*

A pause.

*"Because I won't stay if you do."*Final. Defined.

Final and defined—no ambiguity left to negotiate.

He nodded once. *"I hear you."*

She watched him for a moment longer, because hearing wasn't changing—but it was the beginning.

Imani stood, not abruptly and not emotionally, but intentionally.

"Then we'll see," she said.

And this time she didn't walk away out of uncertainty; she walked away with clarity.

And that—that changed everything.

Chapter Twenty-One: Control vs. Vulnerability

Zaria Barrett did not wake up slowly. She woke up on—mind engaged, body aligned, the day already in motion before her feet touched the floor, because control didn't start at work for her; it began the moment consciousness returned.

What she wore. What she allowed. What she withheld. Every detail calibrated to ensure nothing caught her unprepared.

Which was why, standing in front of her mirror and staring at two outfits she did not need to deliberate over—but was—she recognized the shift immediately.

"This is unnecessary," she said quietly.

Because it wasn't about the clothes.

It was about him.

Her phone buzzed on the dresser.

She didn't reach for it right away, because she already knew—then she picked it up anyway.

Malik: *You free later?*

No buildup.

No framing.

No unnecessary language.

Zaria studied the screen, then tilted her head slightly.

"You would phrase it like that."

Her fingers hovered, then moved.

Zaria: *Depends.*

She set the phone down before the typing indicator could appear, because she didn't wait—she controlled.

The response came anyway.

Malik: *On what?*

A small, restrained smile touched her lips.

Zaria: *What you're asking for.*

A pause followed, longer than usual. Then—

Malik: *Time.*

She blinked once, because that wasn't layered or strategic or anything she could reframe—just time.

Her reply came slower this time.

Zaria: *I have that.*

Another pause. Then—

Malik: *Good.*

That was it.

No plan, no agenda, no structure—nothing to negotiate against.

Zaria stared at the screen.

"That's it?" she murmured.

She exhaled slowly, because that unsettled her more than she wanted to admit.

They met later at a place she hadn't chosen, and that was the first disruption.

It wasn't curated, wasn't exclusive, wasn't anything she would have selected if she were designing the experience, and that—that was intentional.

"You don't like this place," Malik said as she approached, his tone calm, already registering data she hadn't offered.

Zaria took the seat across from him, her posture composed, expression neutral, though her eyes tracked everything.

"It's not what I'd have chosen," she replied.

He nodded. *"I know."*

A beat passed.

"Then why are we here?"

Malik leaned back, his hands resting loosely on the table.

"Because you didn't choose it."

There it was.

Zaria held his gaze. *"That's not a reason."*

"It is when you need something different."

Her lips pressed together briefly.

"I don't need different."

"You need control," he corrected evenly.

Her eyes narrowed a fraction.

"I prefer structure."

"Those aren't the same."

"They are when they produce results."

He didn't argue. He looked at her.

And that—that was worse.

"Say it," she said. *"Whatever you're thinking."*

"I already did."

"No," she replied, leaning forward now. *"You implied it. Say it."*

Malik held her gaze.

"You don't know how to exist without managing outcomes."

Silence followed—clean, sharp, unavoidable.

Zaria leaned back slowly, her arms crossing loosely, still composed, but something beneath tightening.

"That's not true."

He didn't rush.

"It is."

She exhaled through her nose.

"I run events. I manage environments where failure isn't an option."

"That's work," Malik replied.

A pause settled.

"What about everything else?"

That was the fulcrum.

Zaria didn't answer right away, because everything else wasn't quantifiable.

"I don't fail there either."

His mouth curved slightly.

"That's not the same as succeeding."

Her jaw tightened.

"You're pushing."

"I'm observing."

"You always do."

"You always avoid it."

That hit.

She looked away briefly, letting her gaze sweep the uncurated space around them.

"This isn't my environment."

"I know."

"I don't function well outside of it."

"That's the point."

She looked back at him.

"And what exactly is the point?"

Malik leaned forward slightly now, his attention fully focused.

"That you don't have to control everything to be okay."

Zaria held his gaze.

"That's easy for you to say."

"Why?"

"Because you don't carry what I carry."

He didn't interrupt, just waited.

Zaria exhaled slowly, her shoulders lowering a fraction—not surrender, but honesty.

"I'm responsible for outcomes, for people, for expectations."

Malik nodded.

"That's what you do."

A pause.

"It's not who you have to be every second."

Something shifted in her expression.

"If I let go, things fall apart."

"Or they get done differently."

She stared at him.

"That's not acceptable."

"It might be," he said softly. *"You just haven't tested it."*

Silence returned, but this time it wasn't sharp—it was open.

Zaria tapped the table once, then stilled.

"Do you ever lose control?"

Malik considered.

"Sometimes."

"And you're okay with that?"

He nodded.

"Yeah."

She exhaled quietly.

"I don't like that feeling."

That was new—unfiltered, unprotected.

Malik's gaze softened slightly.

"You don't have to like it."

A pause.

"But you might need it."

Zaria looked at him—really looked—because that wasn't about events.

It was about her.

And she didn't deflect, didn't restructure, didn't manage. She let the thought exist.

And that—that unsettled her more than chaos ever had.

Chapter Twenty-Two: The Fight That Matters

Maya Reynolds didn't like unfinished conversations.

She preferred things resolved, sentences completed, outcomes named, and stored where they belonged.

Unfinished moments lingered.

They resurfaced at inconvenient times, bringing questions she hadn't answered and truths she hadn't fully admitted.

The one with Andre hadn't lingered.

It had settled—quietly, heavily, without arrangement.

She told herself she was fine with the distance.

Fine with the pause.

Fine with how things had stalled rather than progressed.

She said it often enough that it almost sounded convincing.

But "fine" didn't stop her from checking her phone too often.

It didn't stop her from rereading neutral messages that somehow carried weight.

And it didn't stop her from replaying the moment she'd stepped away before it could turn into something she couldn't manage.

So when she saw him—unexpectedly, in a place neither of them had planned to intersect—she felt it before she had time to adjust.

Andre stood across the room in quiet conversation with someone Maya didn't recognize.

His posture was familiar. His presence unchanged—steady, contained, grounded in a way that didn't shift to accommodate situation.

It irritated her and drew her in at the same time.

She stopped just long enough to register it, then moved.

Waiting would have meant acknowledgment, and she hadn't decided what that required yet.

But he saw her.

"Maya."

He said her name without emphasis or demand.

She turned.

"Andre."

No smile.

No posturing.

Just recognition.

The person he'd been speaking with gave a brief nod and stepped away, sensing the shift without needing explanation.

And suddenly, there were no buffers left.

"You've been quiet," Andre said.

Maya tilted her head slightly.

"So have you."

A pause followed.

"I wasn't the one who left."

The statement landed cleanly.

Maya exhaled, folding her arms loosely—not defensive, not open.

"I needed space."

Andre nodded once.

"You took it."

He didn't argue. Didn't press.

That unsettled her.

"You didn't reach out," she said.

His expression didn't change.

"You didn't ask me to."

She blinked.

"That's not how that works."

"It is for me."

A sharp breath escaped her.

"So you just wait?"

"I don't chase."

There it was again—that refusal to fill space she had created.

"That's convenient."

Andre tilted his head.

"For who?"

She stepped closer, tone sharpening.

"For you. You don't have to risk anything."

His gaze held steady.

"That's not true."

"Then what are you risking?"

He answered without hesitation.

"Letting you choose without me interfering."

The words hit harder than she expected.

"That's not risk," Maya said. *"That's distance."*

"It's space."

"It's avoidance."

Silence followed—dense, unpolished.

"You walked away," Andre said.

"I stepped back."

"From something you didn't finish deciding."

Her jaw tightened.

"You don't get to decide that."

"I don't," he replied. *"But I saw it."*

She exhaled sharply.

"You see everything."

"I pay attention."

"That's not the same."

"It is when you're right."

She held his gaze, frustration simmering.

"You make everything sound simple."

"Because it is."

"It's not," she snapped.

Andre didn't flinch.

"Then explain it."

That forced her forward.

Maya took another step closer, voice steady but charged.

"You want an explanation?"

A pause.

"Fine."

Another beat.

"I don't trust things that feel like that."

Silence stretched.

Andre waited.

"Like what?"

She shook her head once.

"Easy," she said. *"Uncomplicated. Like I don't have to think before it happens."*

He met her gaze.

"That's not a flaw."

"It is when it catches me off guard."

"That's different."

"It's not for me."

Another pause.

"Why?"

Her breath slowed. This part cost her.

"Because I don't move without understanding where I'm headed."

Andre nodded.

"And you didn't understand this."

"No."

"Then why leave?"

She looked away briefly, then back.

"Because I didn't trust myself to stay."

The air shifted.

Andre's expression changed—only slightly.

"That's not about me."

Maya frowned.

"You always do that. You turn it back on me."

"Because that's where it is."

Her jaw set.

"It's not just me."

Andre nodded once.

"Then say that."

Silence held.

Then—*"It's about both of us."*

The words hung between them without relief.

Andre nodded.

"Okay."

Another pause.

Maya spoke again, quieter this time.

"Then why does it feel like you're the one deciding what happens next?"

Andre leaned forward slightly.

"Because you changed the direction."

"That doesn't mean you stop showing up."

"I didn't."

"How?"

"I stayed where you left me."

She didn't answer immediately.

"That's not the same as being present."

He met her gaze.

"I am present."

A beat.

"Right now."

Something shifted—not resolution, not understanding.

Alignment without agreement.

"You're frustrating," she said quietly.

A faint smile touched his mouth.

"So are you."

Another pause settled in.

Then—

"I almost kissed you."

The admission escaped before she measured it.

"I know."

"And I walked away."

"I know."

A pause.

"And you didn't stop me."

Andre tilted his head.

"Did you want me to?"

The question held.

"I don't know."

The honesty surprised her.

Andre nodded.

"That's where you are."

She lifted her gaze.

"And where are you?"

He stepped closer—not filling the space, not leaving it.

"I would've kissed you."

Her breath caught.

"And then?"

"Then we'd deal with what came after."

Simple.

Unpolished.

Risky.

"You really think it works like that?"

"No."

A pause.

"But I think it's worth finding out."

Silence returned—not empty this time.

Maya didn't step away.

She didn't step in either.

She stayed in the space between, aware that staying meant acknowledging something without naming it.

Because this—whatever it was—didn't end with an answer.

It hung there.

And for once, neither of them walked away.

Chapter Twenty-Three: Running Again

Nia Jackson didn’t leave slowly.

She left clean, with no prolonged conversations, no softened edges, and no emotional residue left behind for anyone else to step around, because that was how she protected herself and how she stayed in control.

So after the weekend that had stretched far past her rules—past containment and past intention—she did what she always did when something crossed into unfamiliar territory.

She reset.

Monday arrived with structure—work, movement, precision—and her shift unfolded exactly as designed: focused, efficient, contained. She moved decisively, her presence untouchable and her attention anchored to outcome and procedure

No distractions, no space for drift, no room for anything that required feeling instead of function.

Her phone stayed silent, not because nothing came through, but because she didn’t look—though she felt it anyway, the pull, the question, the choice she refused to name.

So she didn't check, didn't engage, didn't respond, because responding would make it something again, and she wasn't ready for that.

Tuesday followed the same pattern—routine, control, distance—but by Wednesday this wasn't a reset anymore.

It was avoidance.

Her phone vibrated in her locker as she changed out of her scrubs, the sound cutting too sharply through the quiet room.

Her body stilled for half a beat before she reached for it, though she didn't open the screen because she didn't need to.

Jordan.

She locked the phone again, slid it into her bag, and closed the locker.

"Not today," she said.

The words didn't land.

Outside, the air was cool, the evening suspended between motion and stillness, the kind of calm that usually let her shed whatever didn't belong—but not tonight.

She walked too fast, her steps sharper and her thoughts louder than she wanted.

"You're running."

The voice stopped her—flat, clear, unmistakable.

She didn't turn, because she already recognized it.

"Don't do that," she said, her tone steady and strained just enough to reveal unease.

"Do what?"

She turned slowly. Jordan stood several feet back, his hands in his pockets, posture relaxed and gaze trained fully on her.

"Show up where I am," she said.

He tilted his head slightly.

"I didn't show up."

A pause followed.

"I was already here."

That irritated her more than she wanted to admit.

"Don't play with words."

"I'm not."

Silence—because he wasn't.

"You've been avoiding me."

Nia exhaled sharply.

"I've been working."

He didn't flinch.

"That's not the same thing."

"It is for me."

He stepped closer, not invasive, just present.

"It's not."

Her jaw tightened.

"You don't get to define me."

"I'm not defining you," he said. *"I'm recognizing a pattern."*

She shook her head.

"You always do this."

"You always leave."

That landed harder this time, because it wasn't new—it was repetition.

"I told you I don't stay."

"And I told you I'm not asking you to."

She held his gaze.

"Then what do you want?"

There it was—direct and unavoidable.

"I want you to stop pretending this doesn't matter."

She laughed, short and sharp.

"It doesn't."

He stepped closer again.

"Then why are you still here?"

Silence followed, because that wasn't easy to dismiss.

"I don't argue," she said.

"You are."

Her shoulders dropped, then tightened again.

"You're making this bigger than it is."

"Or you're making it smaller."

That line again—that same pressure.

She looked away, scanning the street and the movement around them, anything that didn't require staying in this exact moment.

"You don't understand how I move."

"Then explain it."

"I don't need to."

"You do if you expect me to accept it."

That shifted something, because now it wasn't just about her.

"You don't have to accept anything."

"I do if I'm part of it."

Her breath slowed, because that was the problem—he was standing inside something she hadn't named.

"I didn't ask you to be," she said.

He nodded once.

"I know."

A pause followed.

"But I am."

Silence settled—clean and firm.

"I don't build things that don't last," she said quietly.

"Then don't build."

A beat.

"Experience it."

She stared at him.

"That's not how I work."

"I know."

"And you're okay with that?"

He shrugged lightly.

"I'm okay with what's real."

That hit, because whatever this was, it had weight.

"You don't get it," she said, softer now.

"Then help me understand."

She inhaled slowly.

"If I let this be something, I'd have to deal with what happens when it ends."

There it was—bare, unprotected.

"It will end," he said calmly. *"Everything does."*

A pause followed.

"That doesn't make it less worth having."

She shook her head.

"It does for me."

"Why?"

"Because I don't recover halfway."

Jordan's expression shifted just enough.

"Then don't do it halfway."

Silence followed, because that option was something she hadn't made space for.

"Or don't do it at all."

She looked at him—still, clear, open.

"You don't make this easy."

A faint curve touched his mouth.

"I'm not trying to."

A pause.

"I'm just not letting you disappear without acknowledging what this is."

That was the difference. He wasn't holding her and he wasn't chasing her—he was standing there, not leaving, and somehow that made running harder.

Nia exhaled as her shoulders lowered, not surrender and not peace, but a subtle release she didn't correct.

"I'm not promising anything."

He nodded.

"I didn't ask you to."

A pause.

"Just don't pretend it's nothing."

Nia met his gaze, then nodded once—small but undeniable.

Because this time she didn't walk away.

And that—that mattered.

Chapter Twenty-Four: The Group Fractures

The group chat had always been a place of release.

Not performance.

Not pressure. Just truth filtered through humor, sharpened by familiarity, softened by time.

It was where they vented first and made sense of things later, where moments that felt too heavy alone could be held together without ceremony.

Until now.

It started the way it always did—with a single message.

Zaria: *I need to talk.*

Maya saw it first.

Her phone lit beside her laptop as she sat cross-legged on the couch, work open but untouched.

She read the message once, then again.

Maya: *That sounds serious.*

The typing bubbles appeared almost immediately.

Nia: *It is.*

That caught her—Nia didn't label things lightly.

A beat passed.

Imani: *I'm here.*

The air shifted, quiet but unmistakable.

Zaria didn't reply right away. When she did, it wasn't a voice note.

It was text.

That alone mattered.

Zaria: *I don't know how to do this without controlling it.*

Silence followed—not confusion, but recognition.

Maya: *Do what?*

A pause. Then—

Zaria: *Him.*

Nia leaned back against her couch, phone loose in her hand.

Nia: *Malik?*

Zaria: *Yes.*

Imani didn't respond immediately. She read it, absorbed it, waited.

Maya: *That sounds like a you problem.*

Zaria replied instantly.

Zaria: *It is a me problem.*

That shifted something. Zaria didn't admit things like that casually.

Imani: *What's happening?*

Zaria's response came slower this time.

Zaria: *I don't know how to be in something I can't control.*

Maya sat up. That landed deeper than Malik.

Maya: *That's not about him.*

Zaria: *I know.*

A pause stretched.

Zaria: *But he's the first person who doesn't let me manage it.*

The silence that followed felt heavier.

Nia typed before she seemed to decide what she was saying.

Nia: *That's not a bad thing.*

Zaria's response came quickly.

Zaria: *It is when I don't know what to do next.*

Maya exhaled, instinct rising.

Maya: *You don't need to know what to do next.*

Zaria: *That's not how I operate.*

Imani: *That's the problem.*

Clean. Direct.

Zaria didn't answer right away.

Zaria: *So what... I just let it happen?*

Nia replied without hesitation.

Nia: *Yeah.*

Maya blinked.

Maya: *Since when do you believe that?*

Nia stared at the ceiling before responding.

Nia: *Since I realized controlling something doesn't stop it from ending.*

That settled hard—not theory, not philosophy.

Memory.

Zaria stayed silent. Imani didn't.

Imani: *That's not the same situation.*

Nia's posture shifted.

Nia: *It's close enough.*

Maya's grip tightened on her phone.

Maya: *No. It's not.*

A pause followed.

Nia: *How is it different?*

Maya took a breath.

Maya: *Because Zaria is trying to control something that hasn't even formed yet.*

Another pause.

Nia: *And I wasn't?*

There it was.

Imani: *You were avoiding it.*

Nia sat up.

Nia: *That's not the same.*

Imani: *It is when it stops growth.*

The tone sharpened.

Nia: *Not everything needs to grow.*

Maya: *That's not true.*

Nia: *It is for me.*

The space between messages widened.

They weren't talking about Malik anymore.

Or Zaria.

They were talking about themselves.

Zaria typed again, slower this time.

Zaria: *Can we not turn this into something else?*

But it already was.

Imani: *It already is.*

Maya leaned forward, elbows on her knees.

Maya: *We're not saying you're wrong.*

Nia: *You kind of are.*

Maya: *No, I'm not.*

Imani: *You're all responding from different positions.*

Zaria's reply came after a pause long enough to feel dangerous.

Zaria: *I just asked for help.*

Everything stopped.

The silence that followed wasn't awkward—it was exact.

Maya's next message came slower.

Maya: *You did.*

Another pause.

Maya: *And we gave opinions instead.*

Nia's shoulders dropped.

Nia: *Yeah.*

Imani followed.

Imani: *That's on us.*

Zaria didn't respond. Not immediately.

The chat didn't feel broken.

It felt strained.

Four women. Four stances. Four different ways of moving through uncertainty.

They didn't align.

Zaria set her phone down, gaze drifting as the quiet settled more heavily than before.

She hadn't gotten what she asked for.

She'd gotten something else.

Across the city, Maya stared at her phone long after the conversation ended, discomfort sitting somewhere beneath certainty.

Because maybe they weren't all standing in the same place anymore.

And none of them knew what that meant yet.

Chapter Twenty-Five: Accountability

Devon Harris didn't wake up with clarity. He woke up with weight—not crushing, because he knew pressure, but different, heavier in the places he'd avoided and quieter where he used to distract himself with movement, strategy, and presentation.

Now—there was nothing to manage, nothing to perform, nothing to reframe.

Just truth.

His apartment looked the same, but it didn't feel the same.

The stacks of papers weren't temporary anymore, and the numbers on his laptop weren't projections—they were current, real, unfinished in ways he'd spent too long dressing up as stability.

He stood there with his hands on his hips, breath shallow before finally releasing it.

"No more adjusting it," he said quietly, because that—that was the shift, not external but internal.

His phone buzzed.

This time, he didn't hesitate. He picked it up.

Imani.

He stared at her name longer than necessary, because she hadn't texted after their conversation, hadn't followed up, and hadn't softened anything, which meant the next move was his—not polished, not strategic, but intentional.

His thumbs moved.

Devon: *I'm not where I said I was.*

He stared at the message, then sent it with no buildup, no cushioning, and no delay.

Across the city, Imani sat at her table with her laptop open, posture aligned, the calm focus she only had when things were internally ordered.

Her phone lit. She glanced at it, read the message once, then again.

Her expression didn't change, but something beneath it shifted, because this wasn't prompted or forced—this was chosen.

Her fingers moved.

Imani: *I know.*

Simple.

Clear.

Devon exhaled softly.

He typed again.

Devon: *I'm still building. Still stabilizing. Still trying to scale without losing everything I've started.*

He paused, then added—

Devon: *I should've said that from the beginning.*

Sent.

No edits.

No positioning.

Imani leaned back slightly, her eyes steady on the screen—not analyzing, but assessing, because this wasn't the version or the presentation.

This was the reality.

Her fingers hovered, then moved.

Imani: *Why now?*

Devon didn't hesitate.

Devon: *Because you were right.*

A pause.

Devon: *And because I don't want to keep doing it that way.*

Imani's eyes softened just enough to acknowledge the shift, but it wasn't enough—not yet.

Imani: *Saying it and living it are different.*

Devon nodded to himself.

Devon: *I know.*

Another pause.

Devon: *So I'm starting with saying it.*

That—that mattered.

Imani exhaled softly, her fingers resting at the edge of the table.

Imani: *And what does living it look like?*

Devon leaned forward, his elbows resting on his knees, phone loose in his hands, because this required more than words.

Devon: *It looks like not positioning myself as something I'm not.*

A pause. Then—

Devon: *Even if it costs me opportunities.*

That was the line.

Imani read it slowly, because now this wasn't about honesty—it was about consequence.

Her fingers moved.

Imani: *That's where most people stop.*

Devon's mouth curved faintly.

Devon: *I'm not most people.*

She let the words sit, then replied.

Imani: *We'll see.*

There it was—not rejection, not forgiveness, but space, deliberate this time.

Devon stood and moved toward his desk, his gaze settling on the laptop, the numbers, the truth he'd reshaped for too long.

He opened it and didn't adjust anything or smooth the edges.

He just looked.

Because this—this was where accountability started, not with her, but with him.

Across the city, Imani closed her laptop, her posture easing just slightly, because now she had something real to evaluate—not potential, not promise, but truth.

And truth didn't need interpretation.

It needed consistency.

She moved to the window, her reflection faint against the glass.

"Show me," she murmured, because words were only the beginning, and this time she was watching for what came next.

Chapter Twenty-Six: Softening Edges

Zaria Barrett did not know how to arrive without preparing.

Even now—standing before the mirror and adjusting something that didn't require refinement—she felt the familiar impulse to align, correct, and ensure every detail was intentional before stepping into a moment.

But this—this wasn't an event.

This wasn't a client.

This wasn't a space she controlled.

And that—that still unsettled her.

Her phone rested on the counter behind her, screen dark, while her mind replayed her last conversation with Malik—not what he'd said, but how he'd said it: the way he hadn't pushed, the way he hadn't retreated, the way he'd left her with something she couldn't organize into a plan.

You don't have to be that all the time.

She exhaled slowly.

"I don't know how not to be," she murmured.

Her phone lit.

Malik: *You on your way?*

No assumption.

No pressure.

Just presence.

Zaria turned, picked up the phone, and studied the message a beat longer than necessary before replying.

Zaria: *Yes.*

Sent.

No qualifiers, no adjustments—nothing to revise or explain.

She grabbed her bag and left before she could overthink the decision.

The place Malik chose wasn't unfamiliar, but it wasn't hers either—quiet and intentional, with enough structure to feel deliberate but not curated enough to feel controlled.

Balanced.

She noticed that immediately.

"You're early," Malik said as she approached.

Zaria slid into the seat across from him, placing her bag beside her chair, her movements composed but noticeably less sharp than before.

"I don't like being late."

He nodded.

"I know."

A pause.

"And I don't like waiting."

Zaria lifted an eyebrow.

"That sounds like a contradiction."

"It isn't," he replied evenly. *"It's preference."*

She almost smiled—almost.

They ordered, simple and uncomplicated, and neither of them rushed to fill the space.

Which was new.

Zaria didn't redirect the silence, didn't frame it or manage it—she let it exist, and that alone was a shift.

"You're different tonight," Malik said.

Zaria looked at him.

"How?"

"You're not controlling the pace."

She exhaled softly.

"I'm trying not to."

He nodded.

"It shows."

A beat.

"It's uncomfortable," she admitted.

That—that was new.

Malik's expression softened just slightly.

"I figured."

Zaria leaned back, fingertips resting against the table, her posture still composed but less rigid.

"I don't like not knowing what comes next."

He didn't interrupt or fix anything—he just listened.

"It feels like I'm missing something," she continued, quieter now. *"Like I should be anticipating what happens before it does."*

"You're not missing anything."

She met his gaze.

"It feels like I am."

"That's because you're used to staying ahead."

She let out a breath.

"That's how I stay in control."

"That's how you manage outcomes," he replied.

A pause followed.

"It's not the same thing."

Zaria didn't answer immediately, because she knew that—she just hadn't allowed herself to say it aloud.

"I don't know how to separate them."

Malik leaned forward slightly, his forearms resting on the table, his attention fully on her.

"You don't have to separate them," he said.

She frowned.

"Then what?"

"You recognize when control isn't required."

It sounded simple—too simple.

"It's always required."

He shook his head.

"No. You just think it is."

Her jaw tightened.

"You're saying that like it's easy."

"I'm saying it like it's necessary."

Silence followed, because that landed differently.

Zaria glanced down, her fingertips tracing the edge of the table before stilling.

"I don't like feeling exposed," she said softly.

That was the truth beneath everything else.

Malik didn't react right away; he understood how much it cost her to say that.

"You're not exposed."

She looked up.

"That's exactly what it feels like."

A pause.

"Because you're not controlling how you're seen," he said.

Zaria held his gaze.

"And you're okay with that?"

He nodded.

"Yeah."

"Why?"

"Because I know who I am."

That landed—because she did too; she just curated how it was accessed.

"I know who I am."

"I know," he replied.

A beat.

"You just don't always let people see it."

She didn't respond, because it was true.

The silence that followed didn't feel heavy this time—it felt open.

Malik leaned back slightly, his posture easing.

"Can I say something?"

Zaria looked at him.

"You usually do."

He almost smiled.

"This one matters."

That caught her.

"Okay."

He held her gaze.

"I'm not here to manage you."

A pause.

"I'm here to be with you."

That shifted everything.

Zaria's breath slowed, because that wasn't expectation or pressure or control—it was choice.

"And what does that require?" she asked.

"Presence."

A pause.

"Not perfection."

Zaria stared at him, because that was everything she didn't allow herself.

"I don't know how to do that."

He nodded.

"Then learn."

Simple.

Clear.

Uncomplicated.

Zaria released a quiet breath as her shoulders lowered—not collapsing and not giving in.

Softening.

"Okay."

And this time she meant it, because she wasn't fixing the moment—she was letting it exist.

And that—that was new, unfamiliar, and real.

Chapter Twenty-Seven: Choosing to Stay

Nia Jackson didn't wait for things to fall apart.

She left before they could, because that was the pattern—the protection—the kind of control she trusted.

If she didn't stay long enough to attach, she didn't stay long enough to lose.

Simple, effective, unchallenged—until now.

She sat on the edge of her bed, her phone loose in her hand, her gaze unfocused as the silence in her apartment stretched longer than usual.

It wasn't uncomfortable, just… loud, because this time she wasn't being pushed away.

She was being asked to choose.

Her phone lit up.

Jordan: *You free?*

Nia stared at the screen, not startled and not rushed, just aware.

Three days ago, she would've ignored it.

Two days ago, she would've replied safely.

Yesterday, she would've answered without commitment.

Today—she didn't move, because the question wasn't what she was going to say.

It was why she hadn't already left.

Her fingers hovered, then stilled.

"You don't stay," she murmured.

That rule had always been enough. Now it felt incomplete, because staying wasn't the danger.

Fear was.

She leaned back against the headboard, her eyes closing briefly.

"If I stay, I have to feel it."

And feeling it meant risk, attachment, loss—everything she'd built her life around avoiding.

Her phone buzzed again.

Jordan: *Or not. Just checking.*

That landed differently, because he wasn't waiting, wasn't pushing, and wasn't trying to anchor her to anything.

He was just—leaving the decision where it belonged.

Nia sat up, her shoulders squaring not from control, but from clarity.

"I'm not running," she said quietly—not to him, but to herself.

Her thumbs moved.

Nia: *I'm free.*

Sent.

No delay, no qualifiers, no exit strategy—nothing to retreat behind.

Across the city, Jordan read the message once, then again, with no surprise and no relief—just steadiness.

Jordan: *Come through.*

No buildup.

No pressure.

Just space.

Nia stood, grabbed her keys, and left.

The walk felt different—not rushed and not calculated, but intentional—and that changed everything.

When Jordan opened the door, nothing about him had shifted: the same presence, the same calm, the same way of inhabiting a moment without trying to control it.

"You came."

She stepped inside.

"I did."

The door closed, and this time she didn't look for an exit.

They didn't rush or pad the space with conversation, and they didn't pretend the shift hadn't already happened, because it had.

"You're not leaving tonight," Jordan said.

Not a question.

Nia met his gaze.

"No."

The word settled between them, different than before.

He nodded once.

"Okay."

That was all—no emphasis, no demand, just acceptance, because this wasn't about convincing her.

It was about her choosing.

They moved through the evening differently—slower, more aware, each moment acknowledged instead of rushed past.

Nia didn't hold back entirely, but she didn't detach either.

She stayed present through the quiet, didn't disappear when things softened, and didn't pre-plan her exit.

At some point, she noticed it—the difference.

She wasn't calculating departure.

Wasn't managing expectation.

She was just there.

And that was new.

"You're thinking again," Jordan said.

She smiled, small and unguarded.

"Not like before."

He tilted his head slightly.

"How?"

She looked at him.

"Before, I was figuring out how to leave."

A pause.

"Now?"

She exhaled softly.

"I'm figuring out how to stay."

That landed—not heavy, just honest.

Jordan didn't move or define it; he just stayed with her.

Because that was enough.

Later, as the night settled and the city quieted around them, Nia lay still.

Her mind wasn't racing, wasn't planning, and wasn't preparing an escape.

She was present, and it didn't feel dangerous.

It felt deliberate—a decision she made, one she owned, one she didn't run from.

Because this time—she stayed.

And that changed everything.

Chapter Twenty-Eight: The Final Test

Not every relationship broke loudly.

Some didn't fracture or collapse or announce themselves as endings.

Some were tested quietly—in timing, in restraint, in whether words became behavior when nothing required performance.

For all four of them, this was that stretch of time.

Imani & Devon

Imani didn't check in. She watched.

That had always been her way.

Words could be arranged.

Intent could be presented.

Even effort needed time before it meant anything.

Consistency had shape.

It repeated. It held.

Three days passed. Then four. Then five.

Devon didn't disappear.

He didn't resurface with justification or reassurance.

He didn't explain what she should feel or ask what she needed.

He stayed visible.

A message arrived late afternoon.

Devon: *I lost a potential client today.*

Imani read it without reacting.

After a moment, she replied.

Imani: *Why?*

A pause followed.

Then—

Devon: *Because I told them I wasn't fully scaled yet.*

The words sat there without correction.

No framing.

No adjustment.

Imani leaned back slightly in her chair.

Imani: *And you're okay with that?*

Devon: *No.*

Another pause.

Devon: *But I'm more okay with that than I am with lying about where I am.*

She reread the message once, then set the phone down.

She didn't respond right away.

Not because she was unsure—but because this wasn't something to answer.

It was something to watch.

Zaria & Malik

Zaria didn't cancel.

That was the first difference.

The second was quieter—she didn't plan.

No layered expectations.

No mental agenda tucked behind competence.

She arrived with only what was present.

Malik noticed immediately.

"You're not managing this."

Zaria sat across from him, posture still composed but less rigid.

"I told you I wouldn't."

A pause.

"That doesn't mean I'm comfortable."

Malik nodded.

"I didn't expect you to be."

She absorbed that without deflection.

After a moment, she spoke again.

"I had a situation at work today."

Malik leaned forward slightly.

"And?"

Zaria exhaled.

"I didn't step in immediately."

She said it evenly, as if describing logistics.

"I let someone else handle it."

A pause followed.

"And?" he asked again.

Zaria met his eyes.

"They handled it."

Silence settled—not tense, not triumphant.

"You didn't lose control," Malik said.

Zaria shook her head once.

"I shared it."

She didn't elaborate, and he didn't ask.

Maya & Andrew

Maya didn't avoid him this time.

That alone marked change.

But she didn't rush toward clarity either.

She met him where she was—not ahead, not behind.

After a few minutes, she spoke.

"I've been thinking."

Andre nodded.

"I figured."

A pause.

"I don't like not knowing what something is."

He didn't interrupt. Didn't define it for her.

"Then don't define it yet."

Maya released a breath.

"That's not how I work."

"I know."

Another pause.

"But that doesn't mean it's wrong."

She studied him for a long moment.

"Or right," she said.

Andre nodded once.

"Exactly."

Silence settled between them without pressure.

Then—

"I'm not walking away."

She didn't frame it as promise or proof.

Just fact.

Andre's expression didn't shift much, but he exhaled.

"Good."

Nothing else followed.

It was enough for the moment.

Nia & Jordan

Nia didn't hesitate.

She showed up again. And again.

Not perfectly.

Not without instinct tugging backward. But she stayed.

One evening, Jordan glanced at her and spoke without emphasis.

"You're still here."

Nia looked at him, posture easy, presence unguarded.

"I told you I would be."

A pause.

"That's new," he said.

She smiled.

"Yeah."

She didn't explain it.

She didn’t need to.

The Shift

Four women.

Four connections.

All standing at the same edge—not resolved, not certain, but tested.

Not by chemistry.

By consistency.

Not by potential.

By choice.

The group chat stayed quiet that night—not fractured, not distant.

Just still.

Each of them felt it—the weight, the change, the way things no longer sat in theory.

And none of them rushed to name it.

They let it remain unfinished.

Let it show itself.

Let it move forward only as far as it could be held.

Chapter Twenty-Nine: What Are We?

There comes a point when movement isn't enough.

When showing up no longer substitutes for clarity, and presence—no matter how steady—leaves something unanswered between two people.

The question doesn't rush or demand to be spoken, but it stays suspended, reshaping every interaction until it can no longer be avoided.

What are we?

Not asked casually.

Not asked for reassurance.

Asked only when the answer carries weight.

Imani & Devon

Imani didn't ask the question directly.

That wasn't her way.

She positioned it.

They sat across from one another, the space between them no longer fragile but not claimed either.

Devon felt different now—not refined away to a version, not managed toward impression.

Present, in a way she noticed without labeling.

"You've been consistent," she said.

It wasn't praise.

It was data.

Devon nodded once.

"I said I would be."

She studied him a moment longer.

"And if it costs you again?"

He didn't hesitate.

"Then it costs me."

The answer wasn't comfortable.

It didn't close anything. But it didn't retreat either.

Imani leaned back slightly.

"I don't build on potential."

Devon nodded.

"I know."

Silence held—unforced, unfilled.

"So what are we doing?"

There it was.

Devon met her gaze.

"We're building something."

She didn't react.

"And if it's not stable yet?"

"Then we stabilize it."

A pause followed.

"Together."

The word changed the temperature of the room.

Imani didn't answer immediately.

"Then we continue," she said finally.

"And we pay attention."

Not reassurance.

Not promise.

Devon nodded once.

"That works for me."

Zaria & Malik

Zaria had learned how to tolerate ambiguity.

She didn't stay there.

"I don't like not knowing where this is going," she said, voice steady, the edge softened but intact.

Malik leaned back, unhurried.

"Then ask what you want to know."

She exhaled, because the question had already been shaping itself.

"What are we doing?"

Malik answered without delay.

"Spending time together."

Zaria blinked.

"That's not an answer."

"It is."

A pause stretched.

"You want a definition."

She nodded.

"Yes."

Malik leaned forward slightly.

"I'm not steering this toward an outcome."

Her jaw tightened.

"I'm not asking you to."

"You are," he said gently. *"You just call it structure."*

The words landed without cruelty.

Zaria inhaled.

"I need to know I'm not investing in something that disappears."

Malik met her gaze.

"You're not."

A pause followed.

"And I won't."

It wasn't a label.

It wasn't a plan.

But it wasn't nothing.

"Then we keep going," she said.

Malik nodded.

"That's what I'm doing."

For the first time, she didn't need more than that.

Maya & Andre

Maya didn't hate the question because it confused her.

She hated it because it didn't.

"What are we?"

Her voice came quieter than before. Less guarded. No deflection.

Andre studied her.

"Do you want an answer," he asked, *"or a direction?"*

She didn't hesitate.

"Both."

He stepped closer—not crowding, not retreating.

"We're figuring it out."

Maya exhaled.

"That's not enough."

His expression didn't change.

"It is if you're staying."

That pulled the truth out of her.

"I am staying."

The words surprised her, but she let them stand.

Andre nodded.

"Then we don't rush it."

A pause followed.

"We let it take the shape it actually has."

She searched his face.

"And if I need more than that?"

His answer came without strain.

"Then you say so."

Simple.

Clear.

Maya nodded once.

"Okay."

Not certainty.

Not relief.

Permission.

Nia & Jordan

Nia delayed asking because asking meant admitting impact.

One night, Jordan spoke first.

"You're not going anywhere."

It wasn't phrased as reassurance.

She met his eyes.

"That wasn't a question."

"No."

A pause.

"It wasn't."

Silence settled between them.

Then—

"What are we?"

Jordan didn't hesitate.

"Not casual."

Her breath shifted.

"That's not a label."

"It's accurate."

A pause followed.

"You stay."

The words landed because she did.

"I don't want to pretend this is nothing."

"I'm not pretending," she said.

He looked at her.

"Then what are we?"

The question came back to her without pressure.

She exhaled.

"Something that matters."

Not clean.

Not finalized.

True.

Jordan nodded.

"That works."

What Was Answered

Four women.

Four connections.

Different rhythms.

Different risks.

None of them walked away with certainty.

None of them pretended the question was finished.

But none of them were standing outside it anymore, either.

The answers weren't settled.

They were chosen—provisionally, deliberately, with eyes open.

And for now, that was enough.

Chapter Thirty: Entangled Frequencies

Not everything ends with a grand gesture, and not everything needs a dramatic declaration, a perfect moment, or a neatly tied resolution that answers every question.

Some things end…by continuing.

Because what they built—was never meant to stop.

Imani & Devon

Imani didn't rush trust; she allowed it.

Weeks passed, not quickly and not slowly, but intentionally, and Devon showed up exactly as he said he would—no regression, no quiet return to old habits disguised as growth.

Just—consistency.

One evening, seated across from her, his tone calm and unembellished, he spoke.

"I secured two clients this week."

Imani looked at him.

"How?"

"Honestly."

A pause.

"I told them exactly where I was."

That mattered more than the outcome. She nodded slowly.

"And they still said yes."

A faint curve touched his mouth.

"They said they respected it."

Imani exhaled, because respect was built that way—not presented, but earned.

"We're building something," she said.

Devon nodded.

"Yeah."

A pause.

"Together."

And this time there was no hesitation in that word.

Zaria & Malik

Zaria didn't become someone else.

She didn't lose her structure or abandon control—she refined it.

Seated across from Malik, her posture composed but no longer rigid, she spoke.

"I delegated today."

He raised an eyebrow.

"Voluntarily?"

She rolled her eyes.

"Yes."

A pause followed.

"And?"

She exhaled, almost surprised.

"It worked."

That still unsettled her.

"You didn't lose anything," Malik said.

She shook her head.

"No."

A pause.

"I gained time."

That shifted the axis, because control was no longer the objective—balance was.

"You're different," Malik observed.

Zaria met his gaze.

"No."

A pause.

"I'm just not holding everything so tightly."

He nodded.

"That's the difference."

And she didn't feel exposed—she felt free.

Maya & Andre

Maya didn't define it; she lived in it.

One evening, standing beside Andre as the city breathed quietly behind them, she spoke.

"I didn't plan this."

He glanced at her.

"I know."

A pause.

"I usually do."

He nodded.

"I know that too."

She released a soft breath.

"But this..."

She hesitated.

"I didn't overthink it."

That was everything.

Andre stepped closer.

"And?"

She met his eyes.

"And I didn't run."

Simple.

Uncomplicated.

True.

His gaze softened.

"That's enough."

And—it was.

Nia & Jordan

Nia didn't promise forever; she promised presence, which felt larger.

One night, his voice steady, Jordan remarked—

"You're still here."

She glanced at him, her body relaxed in a way that no longer felt temporary.

"I am."

A pause.

"That's new."

She smiled.

"Yeah."

Because staying wasn't a question anymore—it was a choice, one she made every day, without planning an exit or rehearsing departure.

Just—being there.

And for her—that was everything.

The Frequency

Four women.

Four relationships.

Different paths.

Different patterns.

Different truths.

But one thing bound them all: they stopped trying to control outcomes, stopped defining everything before it existed, and stopped running from what felt real simply because it wasn't predictable.

And in that space something formed—
not perfect, not guaranteed, not without challenge, but real, entangled, moving, alive.

Because love, especially the kind found later—wiser and deeper—wasn't about perfection.

It was about presence, about choosing each other again and again without needing to know exactly how it would end, only knowing—
it was worth experiencing.

And that—that was enough.

The End

Continue the journey within the Platinum Chocolate Universe, where every story reveals another layer of love, resilience, truth, and survival.

The Platinum Chocolate Universe is a growing collection of interconnected stories celebrating love, resilience, friendship, healing, and the beautifully layered lives of grown people finding their way through the world.

Wherever you begin, every story opens the door to another.

The Ebony M. Elite Series

Friendship. Romance. Sisterhood. And the unforgettable adventure of women rediscovering love later in life.

Start with:

• *Caramel and Steel*

Companion Coloring Book: *Caramel and Steel Line Art*

Continue with:

• *Searching for Platinum Chocolate*

Companion Coloring Book: *Searching for Platinum Chocolate Line Art*

Next in the series:

- *When the Chat Paused* — May 1, 2026

The Rhythm Series

A soulful romance shaped by music, faith, ambition, and the kind of love that grows stronger through time.

Start with:

- *Rhythm & Design*

  Companion Coloring Book: *Rhythm & Design Line Art*

Continue with:

- *Rhythm's First Lady*

  Companion Coloring Book: *Rhythm's First Lady Line Art*

Then discover the emotional continuation:

- *When Love Learns to Heal*

  Reflective Companion: *When the Heart Learns to Heal*

The Run Series

A powerful family saga exploring loyalty, survival, love, and the complicated bonds that shape a lifetime.

Start with:

• *Flip & Run*

Companion Coloring Book: *Flip & Run Line Art*

Next in the series:

• *Just Run* — April 1, 2026

Companion Coloring Book: *Just Run Line Art*

Stand-Alone Platinum Chocolate Romances

Stories of love, rediscovery, and the courage to begin again.

• *The Colors of Us*

Companion Coloring Book: *The Colors of Us Line Art*

• *A Heart's Anchor*

Companion Coloring Book: *A Heart's Anchor Line Art*

• *Cotton Sheets and Velvet Dreams*

Companion Coloring Book: *Cotton Sheets and Velvet Dreams Line Art*

Wherever you begin, the story continues.

— **LongTemple**

www.ingramcontent.com/pod-product-compliance
Lightning Source LLC
LaVergne TN
LVHW010652110826
845149LV00014B/3048